BLACKFIN SKY

KAT ELLIS

RP|TEENS

Philadelphia • London

Books published by Running Press are available at special discounts for
bulk purchases in the United States by corporations, institutions, and other
organizations. For more information, please contact the Special Markets
Department at the Perseus Books Group, 2300 Chestnut Street, Suite 200,
Philadelphia, PA 19103, or call (800) 810-4145, ext. 5000, or
e-mail special.markets@perseusbooks.com.

ISBN 978-0-7624-5401-3
Library of Congress Control Number: 2014933663

E-book ISBN 978-0-7624-5554-6

9   8   7   6   5   4   3   2   1
Digit on the right indicates the number of this printing

Cover and interior design by T.L. Bonaddio
Edited by Lisa Cheng
Typography: Baskerville, Envy Code R, Hustlers Rough, Mesquite,
MPI Delittle, Rock Salt, Willow, and Wood Type

Published by Running Press Teens
An Imprint of Running Press Book Publishers
A Member of the Perseus Books Group
2300 Chestnut Street
Philadelphia, PA 19103–4371

Visit us on the web!
www.runningpress.com/kids

FOR IAN

SILAS'S SPIRIT HAD inhabited the rusted weathervane for many years. From his perch on the school roof, he watched the townsfolk of Blackfin through his empty eye socket as they buzzed through their lives, no more significant than the grains of sand piling up against the shoreline and on the struts of Blackfin Pier.

To Silas, the pier looked like a single raised finger to the visiting whales that had given the town its name. It was the same pier from which a girl had fallen to her death three months earlier—or perhaps jumped, though nobody truly believed that. Either way, the ocean had swallowed her long enough to leech the color from her lips, the breath from her lungs.

The girl—Skylar Rousseau—had been pretty enough, and not completely without brains. But that wasn't the reason behind the town's fascination with her. There was simply something *other* about the girl, though the townspeople were unaware of the extent of their obsession until she was gone.

Silas, being somewhat *other* himself, had found the entire affair a little dull. Having spent his life—and, indeed, his afterlife—embroiled in the happenings of the town, he knew he ought to care a little, but it was just *so* exhausting. With a sigh, Silas turned on his rusted axis to face the ocean.

And there she was.

Skylar raced along the main road without a glance across the bluff. She passed the gnarled oak at the school gates, knocking the old swing that hung from the lowest branch, making it creak with a sound like a baby crying. Her red coat flapped around her legs like dislocated wings.

This girl looked nothing like the pale corpse Silas had seen hauled onto the boards of the pier. Yet she was unmistakably Skylar Rousseau, from her determined frown to her unforgivably ugly boots. It was her, very much her.

Finally, Silas thought, *something interesting.*

But Silas wasn't the only one watching the girl. Standing at the end of the same pier where the girl died, a man shrouded by a long woolen coat observed silently from beneath the brim of his bowler hat.

⁂

BLACKFIN WAS SILENT except for the sound of boots splashing through puddles. Sky was late, the eighth strike of the bell ringing out to scold her from a clock tower whose location in town nobody seemed to know.

Time resumed its normal speed as the final chime dwindled to nothing.

Sky checked her watch as she skirted past the Penny Well, careful not to pass too closely or she'd find all the coins vanished from her pockets.

Eight o'clock. I'm so dead.

She turned into the school gates at a run. Still, she took the time to wave to Silas sitting up on the roof. It was commonly known that failing to salute Silas as you passed would result in foul weather. Besides, courtesy cost nothing, as Sky's mother often reminded her.

Sky opened the front door to the school at the exact moment a gale-force gust took hold of it, slamming it open against the crumbling brick exterior. Every student packed into the hallway stopped, turned, and stared.

"Jeez, who died?" Sky turned from one surprise-slackened face to the next, trying to ignore the eyes creeping over her like cold fingers. She was used to the staring; it would have been impossible not to become a little desensitized to it after sixteen years of incessant gawping. But this was different somehow.

The wind slammed the door shut behind her, but Sky was the only one who jumped.

Sky sidestepped the two youngest Swiveller brothers, whose oversized heads and lurking tendencies perfectly suited their name. One had his mouth hanging open to such a degree that Sky could see the gum stuck to his teeth on one side. She was glad when the gum dislodged and dropped to the floor, breaking his black-eyed stare as he stooped to retrieve it, only to find it had disappeared. The tiled floor of Blackfin High was almost human in its aversion to grime, as though gum and muddy footprints were an affront to the high shine Old Moley had given it with his buffing machine.

Sky spotted a mass of curly hair farther along the corridor, and her breath whooshed out like she'd been holding it for hours. Sean was at his locker, his head dipped to peer inside.

Sky watched her feet instead of Sean until she was standing next to him, which helped untie the knot lodged in her throat. As always, a string of strawberry licorice hung from the corner of his mouth, and as always, Sky snapped an inch or two from the end and started chewing on it.

Normally, Sean would have looked up and made a joke about going in after the stolen licorice, but today he flinched, and she realized he hadn't heard her over his MP3 player.

Sean pulled the buds from his ears, his hand almost seeming to tremble, which was odd.

"Sean," she whispered, quite aware that the other students were listening to every word. "Why is everyone acting so weird? Did someone die?"

Sean reached out as though to brush a strand of hair away from Sky's face, and she willed her expression to read *breezy*, despite the very unbreezy way her pulse thundered. But he didn't sweep her hair aside. Instead he jabbed the tip of one finger at her forehead.

"Hey! What—"

Before Sky could finish, Sean had pulled her into a hug so fierce she couldn't breathe.

"Sean . . . Sean, you're crushing me."

He pulled away from her as though she'd screamed, which she certainly hadn't.

"Where have you been? All this time, I believed you were . . ." Sean turned his back on her and stormed off, his fist banging loudly against one of the lockers as he stalked out the side door.

"Sean!"

She tried to ignore the whispers that started up as the door swung closed behind him, but someone grabbed her arm. Randy Swiveller stared down at her, his face blanched whiter than usual.

"Hey, Randy. I have to . . ."

His eyes stopped her, the bulging orbs boring into her like he wanted something.

"Randy, you're hurting my arm." Sky yanked herself free of his grip. Being hugged by Sean was one thing, but that didn't give Randy Swiveller the right to manhandle her. Sky leveled him with her finest glare.

She didn't wait for his response. She dashed through the fire escape and wiped the unpleasant residue of Randy's hands onto her coat, glad to leave the swell of noise behind her.

⚜

WHEN SEAN HAD first walked into Sky's homeroom two years ago, Sean's grandpa-style cardigan and dorky glasses had made Sky wince in sympathy for the hard time he was going to get in Blackfin High. But Sean had stood at the front of the class, looking as though he knew exactly what the students were thinking, and couldn't give a damn.

I wish I was like him.

That had been Sky's first thought upon seeing his smirk. The second had focused more closely on the interesting contours of his lips, and Sky had promptly taken to hiding behind her hair whenever Sean Vega looked her way. At least, until his sister had become one of her best friends, and made it easier to talk to Sean without her tongue becoming a giant landfill.

Sky hurried across the parking lot to him now, her book bag smacking against her hip with each step and rainwater sloshing over the tops of her pilgrim boots until they squeaked. Sean looked up at the sound.

"So you *are* real," Sean said. Sky had no idea what to say to that, and simply stood watching his fingers clench and unclench around his car keys. "Where have you been, Skylar?"

She met his eyes. He did not look happy. "Stop giving me the *Skylar* treatment, Sean. I don't know what you're talking about, or why those idiots in there were acting like . . . well, idiots. What's going on? Is this some kind of joke? Because if it is, I don't get it. And it sucks. *Hard*."

"It really is you," he said. Sky had the impression a smile lurked somewhere, but it was difficult to say for certain. "But where have you been all this time? Everyone thought you were . . . *I* thought you were . . ." He looked away, rain streaming over his face.

Sky spoke slowly, still trying to fathom what simple thing she must be missing that would make sense out of all this.

"I don't know what you're talking about, Sean. I haven't been anywhere. I've been right here."

He muttered to himself, but Sky only caught the word "coma."

"What date is it?" Sean asked.

"November twentieth."

"And how old are you?"

"You *know* how old I am."

"Just humor me, okay?"

Sky was ready for this prank to be over with. "Sixteen. Sixteen years and three months, to be exact. And you're being ridiculous."

Sean seemed to deflate. "I thought this could all be explained if you'd been in a hospital, sick or something. But that couldn't be . . . Where the *hell* have you been?"

She shivered, hugging her arms. "All right, Sean. Yeah, you got me, you all got me. Ha ha, it was hilarious. Now can you stop being weird?"

Without taking his eyes off her, Sean opened the back door of his Jeep and rummaged around until he found what he was searching for. He stalked over to her, not quite eye to eye. For the briefest moment, Sky thought he was going to kiss her. But as many times as she'd thought that, as many times as Sean had joked about it, he never had.

Jeez.

He wrapped the jacket he was holding around her, his fingers lingering on her hand before he stepped back again.

"Whatever happened to you," he said quietly, "you're safe now. I'm going to take you home, and it'll be all right."

There was something about the quiet intensity of his voice that left no room for argument, although she was still completely baffled by his, and everyone else's, behavior. Sky climbed into the passenger side of his car and said nothing while he drove, the rain beating a rhythm against the windshield like an SOS.

⚜

"YES, MRS. ROUSSEAU, I realize you're at the salon, and I'm sorry to inter—" Sean let out a breath through his nose and closed his eyes. "Mrs. Rousseau, I wouldn't call if it wasn't an emer—" He held the phone away from his ear. When Sky caught his eye, he stuck his tongue out and she laughed. She could hear her mother unleashing a torrent of very unladylike curses.

Sean turned away and put the handset back to his ear.

"You need to come home now, Mrs. Rousseau . . . Yes, I realize that . . . No, I can't tell you why over the phone. Look, I'll see you when you get here . . . Yes, I am in your house. No, I haven't touched your guest towels. I–"

But Sky knew that her mother had already hung up and was no doubt screeching from the salon with foils still in her hair. Her mother had many issues, and Sean was one of them. Or more specifically, the fact that Sean had not grown up in Blackfin was one of them. Yet Sky had always found Sean's non-Blackfinity to be rather appealing. As much as she loved the town whose inherent oddness had spawned the majority of her own, the advent of a newcomer held a certain charm.

Sky's mother could not fathom why Sky had become friends with Sean and his younger sister, Cameron. Lily Rousseau had commented to her daughter on more than one occasion that she should *stick to her own kind*, which did not, apparently, include the Vega siblings, whose parents had sent them to live with their aunt while they took off on an expedition to the Himalayas. The words had bothered Sky immensely, but at the same time, a part of her understood her mother's meaning. In a town like Blackfin, a few idiosyncrasies went unnoticed. Beyond its limits, however, a Black-finite would be subject to far more scrutiny.

Sean set the phone down and smiled wryly at Sky. It faded too quickly. "The last time I spoke to your mom was at your . . ." Sky waited for him to finish, but the sentence seemed caught in his throat. He coughed to clear it, then drew a strawberry lace out of his pocket and chewed on it. Normally the lace would have disappeared in the Blood House either by Lily's machination or the house's own quiet intolerance of junk food. So Sky knew something had to be terribly wrong when it didn't, though Sean appeared too distracted to notice.

"What's going on? Are you feeling okay?" she asked. Even the house was unusually quiet, like it was frozen in shock.

Sean moved slowly to the love seat facing her, sitting with his elbows on his knees and fingers laced in front of him.

"Sky, you fell from the pier and drowned three months ago. Remember, you had your birthday party, then ran off after I . . . Look, I saw your body, watched the ambulance crew try to . . . I watched them *bury* you a week later."

A moment passed. Then another. Finally Sky regained the use of her vocal cords.

"But I didn't fall off the pier. That was just a silly dream, and it was months ago, anyway." She took a breath, let it ease out through her teeth. "This is stupid!" She made a sweeping gesture up and down her body. "I mean, do I *look* like a corpse?"

She immediately regretted being so flippant. This was Sean. There would be a good reason for how he was behaving—Sky would just have to wait until that reason cartwheeled across the room in front of her.

"I didn't drown, Sean. I didn't fall from the pier. It was just a regular-size nightmare that I woke up from *in my own bed.* And I'm fine. I've been fine every day since then. Come on, just yesterday you were teasing me for angsting so hard over midterms. I can't be angsty *and* dead, can I?"

Sky laughed, but Sean didn't join in. He frowned.

"How about I make us some coffee or something while we wait for your mom to get here?" Sean asked. Sky moved to get up, but he shooed her away. "I'll do it. I just need to *do* something."

He disappeared into the kitchen while she sat listening to the sounds of cupboards opening and closing as he searched for cups and coffee granules while the kettle started to whistle on the stove. These sounds of *home* were normally so comforting to Sky, but today they felt off. The kettle's whistle rose unevenly, like someone singing when their throat was clogged with tears.

Sean took a long, long time making the coffee.

❖ 2 ❖

THE LIGHTS IN the Blood House dimmed, flickered, then went out completely. It only lasted a second before they came back on at full brightness, but it was enough to warn Sky of her mother's arrival. When tires screeched to a halt on the driveway, throwing up gravel onto the porch steps, Sean came running from the kitchen and went straight out to meet her with barely a glance in Sky's direction.

"I'm calling your aunt, Sean Vega! You can't just break into someone's house and—"

"I didn't break in, Mrs. Rousseau. The spare key—"

Sean's voice carried smoothly through the open door and her mother's made up for its lack of bass with excessive volume. "I'll have you locked up for breaking into my home. . . ."

Even Sean's sigh was audible. Sky could imagine him closing his eyes as he tried to fight insanity with logic. Her mother had that effect on most people.

"Skylar is inside."

Sky didn't know why this would stun her mother into silence, but it did. For all of five seconds. Just long enough for Sky to drag herself from the couch to the front door. It started to swing shut—the house's way of sheltering Sky from the inevitable Lily-drama—but Sky grabbed the handle and dragged the door back open.

"You DARE use my daughter—"

"Hey, Mom."

Lily gaped at her daughter like she had sprouted tentacles and slapped her with one. All the blood drained from her face, which was a shame as she'd obviously just spent a significant amount of money having it prettified at the salon.

"Mom, do you need to sit down?"

This was too much for her mother, apparently. Lily's eyes rolled back in her head and her body crumpled like a windsock with no breeze. Sky felt it was a testament to Sean's character that he caught her before she hit the ground.

<hr/>

OF ALL THE unpleasant things Sky had imagined her death might involve, there were certain mundanities she had been looking forward to leaving behind. Like her mother's fainting spells.

However, it transpired that she either was *not* dead, or she was the unluckiest ghost in the world.

"I'll get her smelling salts." Sky headed upstairs to search the cabinet in her mother's bathroom while Sean maneuvered Lily onto the couch. Sky didn't know where her mother had acquired the smelling salts, what with it being the twenty-first century, but Lily "fainted" often enough to justify having them.

When Sky returned, she found her mother already somewhat recovered. Sean sat across from Lily while she sipped a glass of water, her hand shaking so badly it spilled onto her skirt. For once, she didn't seem to notice the mess.

"Skylar . . ." Lily's eyes started to roll back again, and Sky darted forward to take the glass from her before she dropped it. A spilled glass of water would put Lily in a funk for days.

"I should call Dad if you're not well. . . ."

"You will *not* call your father!" Lily snapped to attention as though the glass of water had been thrown in her face, her gutter-twang slipping through as she yelled. She huffed for a few seconds before she seemed to remember her fragile state—and her affectations. "Skylar, darling, how are you? What are you doing here?"

Sky's eyes darted to Sean as she tried to think of a good reason for her absence from school. "I, uh, was feeling a little sick, so Sean gave me a ride home."

Lily scowled at Sean. "Oh. You're still here, are you? You can leave now."

"Mom!"

But Sean had already risen to his feet with a grin. "You're looking particularly lovely this afternoon, Mrs. Rousseau. Did you do something new to your hair?" Lily made a noise so quarrelsome it could have passed for a growl. "But you're right, I should leave you two to talk." After one look at Sky's expression, his face softened. "I'll call you tomorrow, if that's all right? I know Cam will have heard about you being back by now, and she'll be dying to see you."

This was all so very strange.

Sky had seen her all of twelve hours ago. Unless she really *was* dead, in which case she had no idea whether the regular laws of time applied.

"Sure," Sky said, not sure how else to respond, and Sean left, the house creaking in sympathy as the door clicked shut behind him. When she turned back to Lily, her mother's eyes were still fixed on the closed front door like she was afraid to look at her daughter.

"What's going on, Mom?" Sky asked, and Lily finally looked up. "You can't think I died, too." She ended with an awkward chuckle.

"Where did you go?"

"Go?"

"You died three months ago, Skylar. Or we all thought you did—the night of your party. And now you show up like nothing happened, I . . ." Sky stared as tears, *real* tears, welled in her eyes. For all of Lily's drama, she tended to hold her tears in reserve for genuinely apocalyptic events, such as Sky's refusal to wear the Dorothy shoes she had presented her with for school.

Or Sky dying, apparently.

Sky took a deep breath. "I'm really not sure what's going on here, whether this is some weird mass hysteria or delusion or whatever, but I am clearly *not* dead, because . . . I'm just not."

Lily stared, her lips forming a tight, thin line. "Then answer this: where have you been since the night of your birthday? Because you certainly haven't been here." Sky was just about to protest when Lily shot any answer she might have given to smithereens. "And who the hell did we bury in the cemetery three months ago?"

❧❦❧

THE DRIVE TO Gui's auto repair shop was short but awkward. Sky wasn't entirely convinced that the whole *dead girl walking* thing wasn't some elaborate prank, or maybe even a dream. After all, she certainly didn't *feel* dead.

How do you know what being dead feels like? She shuddered. *No. I'm not getting sucked into this. Either I'm being punked, or the whole town's gone nuts.*

But Sky knew there was no way her mother would have been able to maintain the charade this long. And Sean just wasn't that mean.

The structure of the auto shop had been cut into the hillside like some kind of dragon's lair, with the only natural light trickling in from the direction of the shore. This meant that Gui always kept several lamps blazing whenever he was inside the shop, spreading warm light across the lot.

As they pulled to a stop in front of the open garage doors, Sky felt a weight lift off her. Her father would set things straight. He always did.

"Gui!" Lily yelled.

Sky gathered she was still in trouble for not being dead. Naturally.

A *bang* came from inside the shop, followed by a muttered curse. Finally Sky's father appeared.

The open doors were easily wide enough for two cars to pass through side by side, but Gui somehow managed to fill the entire space. A huge man by any standards, he seemed even more so as Lily strode over to him, skipping over the puddles in her patent stilettos. Sky slid out of the car and followed her.

"You look good, Lily." Sky heard the soft affection in her father's voice, almost as though he hadn't seen her in a while.

"You were right." These three words were all Lily could utter before Gui's eyes fell on his daughter, and the wrench he had been holding slipped from his fingers.

"*Mon dieu,*" Gui said. Sky bent to pick up the wrench, holding it out to her father. "*Coco?*"

The wrench once again clattered to the floor as Sky was swept from her feet and spun in a circle, her father laughing.

"Daaaad!" Sky shrieked as he spun her again. But it was no use; Gui simply spun her some more.

"I assume you're coming back home now?" Lily said.

There was no obvious emotion on Lily's face, but Sky knew better than to overlook the hopeful gleam in her eye.

"Mom, what do you mean, *coming back*?"

Her father's hand squeezed Sky's shoulder lightly, though it was the light squeeze of a grizzly bear. "None of that matters now, *coco*. Now that you have returned to us, nothing else matters." Gui's eyes filled with tears, his shoulders bouncing as he began to sob loudly.

Unsure of what to do, Sky turned to Lily, expecting to find her examining her nails or rolling her eyes. Instead she was once again swept up into a hug, with one parent on either side sandwiching her in.

"Guys, you're really starting to freak me out now."

❦ 3 ❦

IT SEEMED THAT Sky had only just closed her eyes when she was woken by a hesitant, pounding knock, which could only be her father's.

"Hey, Dad," she called, scrubbing her nest of hair back so she would at least be able to see him.

"How are you feeling, *coco*? A special coffee morning, eh?"

"Definitely."

A few minutes later, a freshly washed and clothed Sky followed the scent of her father's most magnificent blend down into the kitchen, the stairs creaking cheerfully under her feet. Her father hugged her as soon as she stepped into the kitchen. Sky wriggled free, laughing and half-smothered.

"Where's Mom?"

Gui frowned. "She has gone to work at the diner."

Sky couldn't hide her snort. *Considering I just returned from the dead, you'd think Mom could take a personal day.*

"Your mother believes it will be best for us all to get back to normal as quickly as possible. She knows how you dislike being the subject of gossip," Gui said.

Sky thought about that as her father heaped their Saturday pancakes onto two plates and poured them both coffee. She had to give her mother credit for her excuse, even though she suspected Lily's absence had more to do with avoiding Sky's questions.

Sky looked up from her coffee to find her father staring, the kind of stare that said her father was worried.

"What's happening to me, Dad?"

Gui paused with the coffeepot halfway to his cup. "Over the past ninety-seven days, or since you reappeared yesterday?"

Sky thought of the grave in the cemetery and shuddered. "Both."

Gui chewed his pancakes thoughtfully for a moment. "I don't know how to answer that, *coco*. I do not understand it myself."

Sky could tell her father was being deliberately vague, just as she knew that pushing him for answers would achieve nothing except a brisk hair-tousling and a long garble of French to distract her.

"I wish you wouldn't call me *coco*, Dad. I'm not an egg."

Gui winked at her as he refilled the coffee she had somehow drained. "You were once, *coco*." He laughed, easily drowning out Sky's elongated *eeeeeeewwwww* as he put his empty plate in the dishwasher. "Your mama had to work today, but Jared said he would take care of things at the garage."

"Who's Jared?"

Gui froze. "Ah, of course you two have not met. Jared has been working at the garage for a couple of months now. He is a good boy, you will like him. Although he makes me listen to the *death metal*." Gui leaned in, his eyes wide. "I do not like it."

26

Sky took her time chewing the lump of pancake in her mouth. "I can't believe I didn't know you hired someone to work with you at the shop." Then the bizarre truth of her situation hit her, and it left her cold. She knew she wasn't dead, nor had she been lying under the dank soil of Blackfin Cemetery for the last three months. But she'd certainly been *somewhere*, and that wasn't here, at home, with her parents. "I really was gone, wasn't I?"

Her dad wiped his hands slowly on the dish towel. "You really were." Then his beaming smile stole over his face. "Let's go and terrorize some fish."

She didn't respond right away. But Gui's false cheer was hard to ignore for long.

"I will even let you steer!"

SKY HUGGED HER knees to her chest, the first drops of rain just starting to cling to her hair. She watched the rain fall onto Blackfin Lake, but it didn't make any impression on the glassy stillness of the water. The water never reflected anything but the sky, even when Sky leaned over the edge of the boat to try and see beyond the surface.

"Dad, can't we go back in yet? I'm freezing my butt off." She was bored, too, but knew it would hurt her father's feelings to say so. Every few minutes she would catch him glancing her way with teary eyes. She pretended not to notice, and Gui blamed the occasional sniffle on the cold.

"Just a few more minutes, *coco*. I'm sure we will get a bite soon."

Sky waited until her father had turned his attention to his fishing pole before dipping her hand into the icy water. She wiggled her fingers for a moment, and pulled her hand quickly back over the side of the boat, rubbing the heat back into her fingertips.

"*Mon dieu!* Here they come!"

The boat rocked violently as her father stood, and Sky jerked back to avoid toppling over the side. Gui's eyes widened, taking in the dark arrows breaking the surface as the fish swam toward them. Sky felt bad for her part in it—luring in the fish was a trick she'd stumbled across years earlier, though she couldn't have said quite how it worked. She watched Gui set aside the fishing pole and sweep two fish cleanly from the water with his net. Sky looked away while he dispatched the fish with a swift smack to the head.

"It looks like you get your wish after all, *coco*!"

Sky smiled weakly. "Looks like it. Come on, let's go home."

"How about if we head up to Oakridge and see if we can get some pie and hot chocolate?"

"Oakridge is an hour away. Can't we just go home and I'll make us hot chocolate there?"

"I could take you shopping, get some new jeans for your mother to throw out, yes?"

This was a rare offer indeed from the man who had vowed never to set foot in a women's clothing store again after being forced to intervene in Sky's constant fashion battles with her mother. As well as their battles over Sky's hairstyle, Sky being on the chess team, Sky's choice of friends, Sky's refusal to audition for the school play, and pretty much every aspect of Sky's life. So Gui conspiring to buy her a pair of forbidden jeans was beyond suspicious.

"Dad, what's going on? Why don't you want to go home? And why did it seem like you'd moved out when Mom and I came to see you at the shop yesterday?"

Gui sat down, swaying the boat and letting one of the fish they'd caught slide back over the side. "Ah. Well, you see, after you di—uh, *disappeared,* your mother and I weren't getting along so well, and I went to stay in the garage for a few days so we could each have our space. That is all."

Sky peered up at him. "And? Why don't you want to go home *now?*"

Gui spread his hands. "Is there something wrong with wanting to spend time with my little girl?"

"Pah!" Sky rolled her eyes, then handed him the oars. "Take us in, Dad. I'm getting a serious case of frizz here!"

Gui laughed and started rowing, taking them quickly back to the shore.

***

"SO, I CAN go?"

Sky stood with her cell in her hand, brandishing the text message from Cam as though it would add weight to her argument. She'd been surprised to find the cell phone still active after her alleged three-month absence, but a check of the call history confirmed that it hadn't been used in all that time.

But I remember calling Bo and Cam a whole bunch of times!

Nothing was adding up with what Sky remembered—her friends, her parents, even her cell phone were all sticking to the same script. Either she'd just pulled the stunt of the millennium and somehow returned after a three-month dirt nap, or she hadn't. And the way her folks were behaving definitely leaned more toward *hadn't.*

The phone beeped in her hand, making her jump. It was another message from Cam.

Can you come??

When Sky had explained to her parents why it would be an absolutely earth-shattering devastation if she were not allowed to meet up with her friends at the beach bonfire, she had anticipated an argument. Instead, Lily elbowed Gui into silence.

"Have fun, darling."

Nothing would indicate that the couple had been living apart not twenty-four hours earlier. Nothing about them would indicate their daughter had recently returned from the dead, either.

Sky punched in a quick reply, trying not to drop her gaze for more than a second in case her parents made some sudden move. But beyond a shrug from her dad and a smile from her mother, Sky's parents didn't react at all.

I think aliens have replaced my parents. I'll be there in fifteen.

Pocketing her cell, Sky backed out of the room slowly. Then she grabbed her coat and ran.

⚜

THE FLYING FORM of Cameron Vega tackled Sky backward into the sand.

"*Oof!* Jeez, Cam—"

But Cam promptly cut her off with a stream of words so fast and high-pitched that no human could have understood, especially when muffled against Sky's coat. Bo's voice sliced through the din, as she sat with her legs crossed on the driftwood and smoking a skinny roll-up.

"The head cheerleader returns." Bo squinted at Sky through the smoke, not smirking at her scowl as she normally would. There was no cheer squad in Blackfin, and Sky would certainly not have been on it if there had been—at least, not voluntarily. Her only extracurricular credit was her chess team membership, which she tended not to shout about. "Nice of you to call and let us know you're alive. Oh, wait, you didn't."

Sky picked herself up and brushed the sand off her coat once Cam had sprung back to her spot on the log. "Are you guys seriously telling me you don't remember me being here for the last three months?" They stared at her, shredding Sky's hope that her two best friends would put the world back on its axis. "Bo, you don't remember calling me last Saturday to ask me to cover for you when your mom thought you were at my house for a sleepover?" Bo narrowed her eyes. Sky turned to Cam. "Thursday, after that seagull crapped on your sweater, I skipped math to run home and get you a clean one while you hid in the girls' bathroom. Come *on*. I've seen you both practically every day!"

Cam smiled sheepishly. "We really, *really* missed you, Sky."

Bo rolled her eyes, but Sky saw through it.

Bo missed me, too. Oh crap.

"Can't you tell us where you went? We'll keep it a secret, if that's what's bothering you," Cam said.

"Look, I'm not keeping anything secret from you. I just don't know what to tell you guys. I've been right here the whole time. It's not *my* fault you don't remember." Sky held up a sandy hand when Cam looked like she was about to interrupt. "Yeah, I get it. I can't figure it out, and to be honest, I don't even want to right now. I just want to chill with you two and forget the whole thing, just for tonight." She looked from Cam's wide eyes to Bo's slightly arched eyebrow. "No chance of that happening, huh?"

Sky sank down next to them again, throwing a warning look at Cam in case she got any more ideas about taking her down.

"I'm glad you're back, Sky. Even if you say you didn't go anywhere."

Although Sky felt like she had seen her friends only a couple of days earlier, the sincerity in Cam's expression made her feel the absence as though she, too, had lived it.

Bo flicked ash from her cigarette into the small fire. "Did you know your grave's been dug up? I was there yesterday; it's just a hole now."

"What?" Sky almost choked. "It's not *my* grave."

Bo looked at her pointedly. "Your name was on it. That pretty much makes it yours."

"But who dug it up? Why? I mean, I'm obviously not *in* it."

Bo shrugged. "Somebody is. Or was. And I would have thought it would be a police thing, but there would have been tape around the site if it was an official exhumation. I'm betting someone else did it."

Sky turned to Cam. "What did your aunt say?"

Officer Holly Vega was the only cop in Blackfin, and so grounded and matter-of-fact that nobody was ever surprised to learn that she was a police officer. That didn't mean she was well liked, though. The entire population of Blackfin maintained a wary distance from her, as though the skeletons in their closets were spring-loaded and ready to burst out onto the front lawn.

Bo cut in before Cam could answer. "You know we don't talk to the po-po. Besides, she's a cop. She'll figure out she's a corpse short sooner or later."

If Cam was offended by the offhand insult to her aunt, she didn't show it. Sky could tell her brain was focused elsewhere.

"It's almost like you're a zombie and you clawed your way out of your own grave."

Bo took one look at Cam's worried face and burst out laughing. Sky tried to smile, but it felt flat.

"How come you were at my . . . at the cemetery, anyway?" The cemetery lay at the edge of town, nestled between Provencher Street and the steep rise up into the Lychgate Mountains. It was a miniature labyrinth of broken angels, crumbling tombstones, and exactly thirteen black cats—and not even Bo was creepy enough to hang out there by choice.

Bo looked levelly at Sky. "I've been talking to you there for the last three months. I guess it's become a habit."

Bo cleared her throat and turned away.

"Bo!" Cam hissed. "Stop making her feel bad. It's not her fault she didn't die!"

Bo ignored Cam. "So did *you* speak to Cam's aunt yet?"

"Uh, no. Why?"

"You must see how she might be a *little* curious to know what happened to you, seeing as she spent the last three months questioning suspects."

"Suspects?"

"Had to rule out murder, I guess. Nobody really believed *Skylar Rousseau* could accidentally kill herself."

"You're really starting to sound annoyed that I'm alive."

Bo looked away silently, the closest she would ever come to an apology. Cam went on, oblivious.

"You've missed so much stuff going on, Sky! Have you seen the hot new guy who's working with your dad? His name's Jared and he's got this whole goth-pale but with a smokin' hot bod thing going on and like a bajillion piercings—even in his tongue—and the smokiest eyes I ever saw!"

"Yeah, Dad mentioned he had someone working for him now. I guess I'll go check him out soon." Sky grinned. "Unless you're saying he's already off-limits?"

"Pah." Bo's laugh never quite sounded like a laugh, as though she couldn't be bothered putting in the effort to make it convincing. "As if you'd be interested."

"So, what else did I miss?" Sky fidgeted. "I mean, while I was . . . away?"

"Ooh!" Cam smacked her palm against Bo's thigh. "I almost

forgot! The chess club got closed down because they didn't have enough members!"

Why Cam was so invigorated by relaying this piece of news was a mystery to Sky. "Really? But we've always gotten by with six members . . . Oh, right. But it's only been a few months, and I'm back now. Maybe Mr. Hiatt will start it up again."

Bo laughed. "Of course he will, if you ask him."

Sky heard the distant sounds of some of their classmates fooling around farther along the beach. She hadn't realized she was looking for Sean among the fuzzy outlines until he appeared at his sister's back a moment later, holding three cans of soda in a precarious pyramid. Once he'd handed a can to each of the girls, he came and sat in the only vacant log-spot next to Sky. He squeezed her arm for a second, like he was checking she was still there.

Sky popped the top on her soda as she gazed into the darkness where a group of guys was still fishing bottles out from underneath the pier. All manner of flotsam washed up on Blackfin's shores, and there was always an assortment of bottles among it. Whenever they were at the beach, the Blackfin teens would search through the bottles for messages—and would generally find one or two in a good haul. Sky listened to the *clink* of glass in the distance.

"Find anything good?" she asked.

Sean nodded. "One angry letter to Santa. But you can hardly see them now, and the last one Charlie fished out had a dog turd in it. At least I hope it was a dog's." Sky laughed, but Sean stared into the low fire. "Aunt Holly's been trying to reach you. I said I'd call her if I saw you here."

"Sean!" Cam hissed and kicked at her brother, but Sean moved out of the way, ending up almost on top of Sky.

"*Cam.*" He glared at his sister for a second before turning to Sky. "She has to ask you some questions. About where you've been. And stuff."

It was odd to see Sean ill at ease.

"Yeah, Bo mentioned something about that." The ring-pull on Sky's can became a source of fascination. "But I don't know where I've been. I mean, I *do*, but none of you guys believe me."

"I still can't believe you're really here. I mean, *here.*" Sean looked away. "Have your folks taken you to the hospital to get checked out?"

"Hospital?"

Sean looked down at his fingers, elbows propped on his knees. "Yeah. I know that's like a dirty word or something around here, but modern science is kind of *the thing* everywhere else in the world." He cleared his throat. "I mean, so they can test you for drugs. And, you know, check you over."

"She wasn't kidnapped, wingnut. She *died*. We all saw her before they put her in the ambulance. No way was that girl about to get up and run away for three months." Bo relit her roll-up in the edge of the fire. A long draw on her cigarette, and her face disappeared for a moment in the smoke. "This isn't some experiment for you two to puzzle out over heated looks and chemistry books."

Sean leaned back, one palm braced on the driftwood at Sky's back. "I'm open to other explanations if you have one—"

"That's what I'm saying," Bo continued. "There *is* no explanation. Not for this, not in this town."

All four sat in silence for a long moment, except for Cam, who squeaked briefly as she began asking a question before promptly forgetting what she had been about to ask.

Sky finally spoke. "I'll come by to speak with your aunt first thing in the morning. Text me if that's a problem, okay?"

For a while Sky tried to steer the conversation away from herself to more normal things, but it was no use. Her friends continued weaving grand webs of conspiracy to explain her absence, but Sky wasn't really listening. She was distracted by a slithery, dark feeling that something was wrong.

Sky let her gaze drift to the promenade overlooking the beach, and for a moment she thought she saw a man standing up there, just watching.

"Hey, who's that guy . . ."

But by the time Sky looked back from her friends to the spot where the man had been, there was nothing left but shadows.

4

THERE WAS NOT one speck of light to show where she was, but she could feel she was in an enclosed space. Sky lay still for a moment, waiting for her brain to catch up with her surroundings. Was she in bed, or not?

With one hand, Sky tried to reach for the switch on the electrical cord of her bedside lamp, but her fingers knocked up against something hard and smooth. Then her elbow met the same resistance as she tried to reposition herself to feel what it was.

Weird dream.

Her breath bounced back at her, and further exploration showed that there was another barrier only inches in front of her face.

It's like I'm in some kind of crate or something. Or . . .

Realization hit her at the same moment her forehead banged against the underside of the coffin lid.

Sky struggled to get her arms free, feeling the cramped enclosure pressing in on her even more now that she knew where she was.

Not enough space. Can't breathe!

Her breaths were too loud, far too rapid for such a tight space. A space with limited air.

God, it stinks in here!

Sky's fingers caught on something cold and claylike, and she stopped struggling. She stopped breathing altogether.

Oh, please tell me that's not what I think it is.

A flash hit her eyes, blinding her—but not before Sky had an instant to see what she was lying next to in the darkness.

A waxy face with sunken eyeballs lay next to her. A face that looked too much like her to be anyone else.

Another bright pulse of light, like a billion tiny lightning bolts.

Sky shrieked and jolted upright in bed.

She was home; she was safe.

"Is something the matter, darling?"

Sky's mom stood silhouetted in the doorway, the hallway light behind her casting a streak of pale yellow across the carpet.

Sky tried to calm her breathing, the memory of rot-stink still in her nostrils. "No, nothing. Just a bad dream. Sorry if I woke you, Mom."

Her mother closed the door with a gentle *click*, and Sky settled back into her bed. But she had no intention of falling back to sleep—not if those were the dreams she could expect to greet her.

⚜

SKY SNUCK OUT of the house before her parents woke the next morning. She was anxious not to give them an opportunity to run interference, as they certainly hadn't looked happy when she'd suggested going to talk to Officer Vega. But she needed some help figuring out exactly what had happened to her, and who better to help solve the puzzle than the police? Still, she hesitated before knocking on the door of the Vega household.

She wasn't surprised to find Officer Vega already up and dressed. Her black hair was braided back, and the open top button of her police uniform was the only concession to it being the weekend. Officer Vega seemed equally unsurprised to find Sky on her front porch.

"Amazing," Officer Vega said with a smile, standing back to make room for Sky to pass. "If I weren't seeing you with my own eyes, I wouldn't have believed it to be possible."

The house was small and functional, which suited Holly Vega's personality just like the revolver strapped to her hip. At seven o'clock. On a Sunday.

"Uh, yeah. I'm getting that reaction quite a lot." On the short walk over to the Vegas' house, every person Sky had encountered had reacted the same way. Lorenz di Sola out walking his seven dogs, Principal Hemlock jogging up toward the Point, and Old Lady Brady who always sat on the same bench outside the park for an hour each morning—all of them had stopped, gasped, and then hurried off as though Sky were an omen of the apocalypse. Even the dogs. "I hoped I could come talk with you before my folks figure out I'm gone," Sky admitted, following Officer Vega through to the family room and swallowing nervously. She sat on the worn sofa she'd sat on a thousand times with Cam, but now the seat felt a little warmer than ever before.

"Yeah, your mom didn't sound too thrilled about me speaking to you when I called yesterday," Officer Vega said. Lily hadn't even mentioned the call to Sky. "Can I get you a cup of tea?"

Sky cleared her throat. "Uh, no, thanks."

Officer Vega sat in the armchair facing her. "Would you like me to call someone to come over and sit with you while we talk? It would be absolutely fine."

"Not unless I'm under arrest."

Officer Vega didn't laugh, but she gave Sky a small smile. "You're not in any kind of trouble, Skylar. I'd just like to know where you've been. I need to close the investigation, and for that, I need a few answers."

"I'll tell you what I can," Sky said, expecting Officer Vega to begin questioning her. But the police officer just sat back and waited for Sky to begin. "Oh . . . um. Okay. The way I remember it, I had a party with a few friends, it sucked, then I went to bed."

"This was on the night of your birthday, August twentieth?" Officer Vega asked. Sky nodded. "And what about after that?"

"After I went to bed? Nothing." *Except I had a freaky dream where I fell from the pier, but that never actually happened.* "I woke up the next day, had breakfast, and picked up some groceries for my mom. Life went on just like normal."

"You saw your mom the day after your party?"

Sky blinked. "Of course."

"So, am I right in thinking that as far as you remember, you have been living at home with your parents, going to school as usual, and nothing out of the ordinary has happened at all since your birthday?"

Sky nodded. "That's right. Oh, except Bo said that someone's dug up a grave in the cemetery. But that happened Friday, after everyone started acting all weird."

Officer Vega leaned forward. "And why didn't Margaret—I mean *Bo*—report this immediately?" One glance at Sky's expression, and Officer Vega shook her head. "Never mind. I still forget where I am sometimes. I'll drive down there shortly to check it out." Officer Vega pursed her lips. "You realize that nobody else remembers you being here for the last three months." It didn't sound like a question, but Sky nodded anyway. "How do you explain that you remember the last three months happening one way, and everyone else remembers them another?"

Sky was quiet for a long moment. All she could think about was the cold, clammy feeling of the dead body she'd dreamed about the previous night. She shivered.

"I suppose the real question is: why does everyone in Blackfin remember you dying when you clearly did not?" Officer Vega sat back, drumming her fingers on the arm of the chair.

"Weird things happen in Blackfin," Sky said.

Officer Vega nodded slowly. "They certainly do, Skylar. They certainly do."

"What happens next? Is there going to be an official investigation into where I've been?"

Officer Vega pressed her mouth into a straight line. Finally, she shook her head. "Officially, the case will be reclassified as a runaway, and closed. Of course we'll still need to figure out who was buried in Blackfin Cemetery, and how they came to drown just off our beach when there have been no missing person reports in the tri-county area in over a year, and what the hell has happened to that body *if* it's disappeared. But that won't involve you, Skylar."

"What about figuring out what happened on the night of my party?"

An odd expression passed over the police officer's face. "Unless you'd like to report that a crime was committed that night, it isn't a police matter." Sky shifted. There had been no crime committed—at least, none that she remembered—but there had been certain events that she would rather not think about.

"Then I guess you can't help me."

"It seems not. But," Officer Vega added, a new light in her eyes, "maybe your mother can help you figure it out?"

"My mother?"

Officer Vega's only response was an enigmatic smile.

⚜

SKY KICKED AT her bed sheets, stifling despite the autumn air whispering through her window. What *had* happened on the night of her birthday?

"The best way to figure this out is to go back through what happened and pinpoint where your version of events first differs from everyone else's."

That was what Officer Vega had said to her before she left. Sky had been about to ask the police officer what she had meant about her mother, but their conversation had been cut short by the sound of Cam's door opening upstairs.

"Maybe we should continue this conversation some other time."

Sky nodded, even though she'd probably tell Cam everything later, anyway.

Pinpointing where the two versions diverged—that was Sky's first task. She thought back to that night, going through every tiny detail leading up to her birthday party, determined not to miss something that might offer a simple explanation for what had happened. When Sky had reached her room, she had flipped to the blank pages at the back of her chemistry workbook and began to write.

My party started out exactly like Mom planned it. . . .

SKY'S PARENTS HAD rented the high school gym for "the Big Night," as Lily Rousseau had taken to calling it. This had led to some heartfelt sighing on Sky's part, and a good deal of silent eye-rolling on her father's.

Fairy lights, balloons, glitterballs, and streamers—it looked like the Mardi Gras rejects pile had landed at Blackfin High. The lights twinkled and swayed in a breeze that wasn't there. The Blackfin sky had obligingly darkened at precisely eight o'clock to show off Lily's decorations, and no silly little thing like the wind was going to detract from the effect.

"Oh crap."

Sky felt dozens of eyes on her as she kicked at the long dress her mother had made her wear.

Would it be really, truly awful if I ditched my own party?

Sky knew half the people from her class had only come because Blackfin was terminally lacking in entertainment. Others had probably been forced by their parents, many of whom shared Sky's healthy fear of her mother. Everyone who frequented the diner knew from experience that if someone crossed Lily Rousseau, every item on the next day's menu would have a distinctly bitter aftertaste.

No, ditching was not an option.

"Your father and I will be back at midnight to get you kids in order, okay?" Sky looked up at her mom, who was beaming at her. She was beautiful when she smiled.

"Thanks, Mom."

Sky turned and found herself nose to nose with the one person she'd *really* hoped wouldn't show up. But Randy—the creepiest boy in a town full of creepy boys—was right there, grinning at her.

"Happy birthday, Skylar Rousseau. Dibs on the first dance with the birthday girl."

His voice had a phlegmy quality that made her shudder. She tried to cover it with a smile before edging quickly past him.

"I won't forget!"

Sky made a break through the crowd to where Bo and Cam stood waiting near the DJ booth.

"What's going on with Randy Skeeve-alert?" Bo asked, jutting out her chin in Randy's direction. Turning her back so she could pretend that Randy and most of the other partygoers weren't boring holes in her with their eyes, Sky explained the situation with the dance.

Bo snorted, loud enough to be heard over the music. "Who the hell uses dibs for a dance? Does he think he's Mister-Bloody-Darcy?"

"I'd just stay out of his way, if I were you. You can't actually *dance* with him," Cam shouted over the chirpy pop song, which ended just as she added, "HE'S SUCH A DOUCHEBAG."

Bo laughed, which set Sky off, and soon she found that her party didn't entirely suck. Someone graciously spiked the punch, and within an hour the three girls were happily mocking each other's dance moves and rating the kissability of every guy in the room.

Every guy except Sean. Even though Sky kept shooting covert looks his way, she knew he was off-limits. There were only eleven months between Cam and Sean, making Sean the oldest in their grade and Cam the youngest.

Sky watched Sean talking to some of the other guys on the soccer team, trying to lip-read as one of them teased him about something. Sean just rolled his eyes and smiled his cute, lopsided smile. And then he looked up and caught Sky smiling back at him and waved. Sky finger-waved before turning away, heat rising in her cheeks.

"I don't know why you keep shooting him down," Bo's voice pulled her attention back, and Sky saw that Cam had also noticed her watching Sean.

"I don't keep shooting him down!"

Bo's hand shot up. "I call bullshit."

Cam made a show of being upset, even going so far as to stamp her foot. "But *I* was just about to call bullshit!"

"It's a moot point, anyway. Sean doesn't think about me that way," Sky said. Her best friends looked at her incredulously. "What? He doesn't!"

"He joined the chess team, for God's sake. Why the hell would he do that, if not to spend time with you?"

"Maybe he likes chess."

"Nobody actually likes chess," Cam answered, adding before Sky could contradict her, "except you. And no offense, but that's kind of the least cool thing about you."

Bo laughed her hollow bray. Sky's hand had somehow made its way to her hip, and she tried to make it appear casual. "But that doesn't mean anything. So maybe Sean likes me a little. He's never asked me out on a date or anything. Not seriously. And what about Bridget di Sola?"

Bo sighed dramatically. "They went on one date. Besides, you can't expect him to stay celibate on the off-chance that you'll figure out he *has* been serious the zillion times he's asked you out." Sky felt like she'd been sucker punched, but Bo just laughed. "Oh, relax. I'm not saying he screwed Bridget di Sola. I mean, he *might* have— she's pretty much hot to death—but that's not what I'm saying."

Cam rolled her eyes as she leaned in to shout-whisper over the music, "There was no screwing involved, Sky, trust me. He's not like that."

Still, Sky's stomach was a churning mess. It didn't help that she looked up and caught sight of Sean across the gymnasium. The awkwardness was slightly diffused as he appeared to be trying to teach Charlie Volante, Sky's regular partner in the school chess club, how to pop-n-lock. "So, you mean . . . I mean, would you mind if . . . No, no, it would be too weird. . . ."

Cam smiled as she watched Sean, who was trying not to laugh at Charlie popping a dubious set of moves in time with the music. "He's my brother. Seeing him with anyone is weird. But I'll get over it, especially if it's you."

Sky's heart thudded out of step as she caught Sean looking at her. She wanted it to be true. But would someone like Sean really be interested in dating a Blackfin freak like her?

"I dunno. Let's just leave it for tonight, okay?"

"Fine, golden girl. I'm going outside for a smoke." Bo didn't wait for a response before turning on her spiked heels and heading out of the gym.

Cam squeezed her arm. "I really don't mind, Sky. But whatever, that's cool."

Sky tried to put on a convincing smile. She and Cam half danced to another track, but Sky could see Cam watching the door, probably wishing Bo would hurry up and come back.

"Uh, I'm just going to run to the bathroom. I'll be two minutes, I promise!" Cam said.

Sky didn't want to be left standing alone like a loser at her own party. But Cam made the universal sign of needing to pee, so Sky waved her off.

Sky didn't get the chance to dwell on her misfortune before

a hand tugged on her arm, spilling the punch she'd been holding. Black eyes met hers as Randy Swiveller yanked her arm again.

"Come on."

"What are you doing?" Sky tried to twist her arm free, but it was like trying to escape the grip of a hungry squid. A sickly feeling rolled over her as she wondered whether Randy did, in fact, have suckers on his fingers. "Randy, you're hurting me!"

Sky felt Sean standing behind her.

"Randy, get off her."

"This is none of your—"

"And then you can apologize. Do it now."

Sky tensed as she waited for Randy's response. Sean wasn't a big guy, and she'd never known him to get into a fight in the two years he'd lived in Blackfin, but Randy wasn't usually the confrontational type, either. He generally kept his creepiness to dark corners.

Randy slackened his grip on her arm enough that she could tug herself free, but a look at his face told her how much he did not appreciate Sean's interference.

"You're not one of us, Vega. Skylar's not for you!" His words were uncomfortably close to those her mother had used—*you should stick to your own kind*—and Sky felt the need to scrub her skin where Randy had touched it. "But we can talk about this outside if the message isn't getting through your thick head."

Sky was almost afraid to look at Sean, not sure how she'd feel if he backed down, and not sure how she'd feel if he didn't.

"Let's do that."

Sky was shell-shocked as the two stormed out through the gymnasium's side door. Once her brain had rebooted, she followed them outside.

They hadn't gone far. Sky saw them outlined in the clear August moonlight, grappling clumsily with one another, throwing awkward punches and staggering as they landed. It was only when Sky came within a few feet that she was sure which outline was which, though neither seemed to have the upper hand in particular.

"Randy! Stop it!" Sky grabbed his arm to pull him away from Sean. Her hand came away clutching a torn piece of Randy's sleeve, which he looked down at with nostrils flaring—one of which was oozing blood over his lips—and he shoved her, hard. Sky tripped on the hem of her skirt and landed on the pavement.

Before she could recover, there was a wet *thwacking* sound, then a high-pitched wail like a rocket about to go off.

The rocket was Randy. Not quite screaming, but certainly making a noise outside the manly spectrum, he clutched his nose with both hands.

"You hit me!"

Sky got back to her feet in time to see Sean shrug. "We *were* having a fight." Randy's keening rose in pitch and volume, and Sky took an uncertain step toward him.

"Stay away from me, you frigid whore!"

Randy shoved Sky again, and she and Sean both went sprawling. Randy fled, his footsteps and staccato sobs fading long after he'd disappeared from view.

"Sean, are you okay?" He nodded once, eyes still focused on the spot where Randy had stood. "Why did you do that? You didn't need to fight him."

"Seemed like the right thing to do." He gave Sky a half grin, but it turned into a grimace as it pulled at his split lip. Sky used the piece of Randy's shirt she was still clutching to dab at it, then froze when Sean's hand closed over hers. "Sky . . ."

It would have been the perfect moment to kiss him.

But had she? Those same doubts had whirled through her mind—*Does he really like me? Am I about to make a huge idiot out of myself?*—and the moment vanished with them pulling apart and apologizing over nothing.

Except a part of her remembered it differently. Somehow, she also remembered a different version of that moment, where she'd taken a chance and leaned in to kiss Sean. And it had ended with her running, crying like a total fool, to Blackfin pier. *That* seemed to be the reality everyone Sky had seen over the last three days remembered, the moment they'd lived and she hadn't.

The moment she'd stopped living altogether.

❧ 5 ❧

SKY GOT THE same stunned silence in response to her arrival at school as she had three days earlier, but she kept her expression neutral. Heads turned in her direction and rubber soles squeaked to a halt on the tile floor, one ogler even dropping her book bag for extra drama. Sky tried to ignore them, even the Swivellers with their jointless necks following her with their stares all along the hallway to her homeroom.

She took the seat between Cam and Bo, rolling her eyes for their benefit. "Looks like I'm still the freak du jour."

Bo laughed. "When were you not?" Sky scowled. "Really, Sky? I know you never exactly asked for the attention, but the staring is hardly new. You flit around, being all *Skylar Rousseau*, and then act uncomfortable when people stop what they're doing to stare at you. You can't be remarkable without being remarked upon."

"But I'm *not* remarkable." Sky squirmed, and both her friends watched her. Whatever it was that Bo and everyone else in town seemed to see in Sky, she couldn't see it herself. But she knew it was there, and that it *had* to be to cause such a reaction.

"It's like watching someone trying to saddle a cat," Cam chirped.

Bo nodded appreciatively. "Nice analogy."

Cam frowned. "Doesn't an analogy have something to do with your butt?"

"Minus one million points. And she was doing so well!"

Despite the fact that her friends were making fun of her, Sky was starting to feel a little better. After all, this was perfectly normal.

"But, Sky, is it true, what they're saying? Were you actually dead the whole time you were gone? Because you can tell us, you know, if you *were*."

Sky was spared having to answer by the final bell ringing. Mr. Hiatt glared at the students until they stopped talking, but their eyes never left Sky.

Just as Mr. Hiatt began roll call, the door slammed open again and Sean hurried in. Sky watched him mutter an apology to Mr. Hiatt as he took his seat near the front.

"Is Sean okay?" Sky whispered to Cam.

"He hasn't said anything, but I know he's not been sleeping well the last few nights."

"He freaked out when you died, and now he's freaking out because you're back," Bo explained, with a waft of the minty gum she chewed to hide her ashtray breath. "It's obvious."

"Why would Sean be freaking out about that?" At Bo's look, Sky added, "More than anyone else, I mean."

Cam answered, "When you died, it hit Sean really hard. And then there was all that stuff with the investigation."

"Whoa, *what stuff?*" Sky's tone caught Mr. Hiatt's attention, and he turned to glare at her.

"Skylar Rousseau?" Mr. Hiatt said as his eyes widened.

Bo sat back, crossing her ankles in front of her desk. "I guess somebody didn't get the memo."

"But *how?* I mean, how are you *here?*"

"My mom did call Principal Hemlock to check it was okay for me to come in," Sky said.

But Mr. Hiatt was already backing toward the door. "The principal—yes, I need to see the principal."

As the door closed behind him, Mr. Hiatt's footsteps could clearly be heard racing along the gleaming tiled hallway toward Principal Hemlock's office. Once again, Sky felt all eyes turn toward her—not the least of which belonged to Randy Swiveller. Her fingers curled into fists as she remembered how he had behaved at her party.

"What do you want, Randy?"

He smiled, all the gummy spaces between his teeth glistening with spit as he leaned in. "Freak, that's what you are. I know you ain't real like the rest of us."

Bo's eyelids had lowered to half-mast. "Seriously? One of the Swivellers calling *anyone* a freak is just too hilarious. Ha." Sky marveled at how Bo held Randy's stare.

"Our dad says you were probably kidnapped by a pedo," Randy whispered, moistening his lower lip with his tongue. "He said it would have to be a pedo, not a normal raper, 'cause you haven't got any tits."

"You're disgusting," Sky shot back. Her cheeks felt hot enough to melt, and her eyes were trying to leak. She wouldn't cry, though. Not in front of them.

Bo's droll tone banished any thought of tears. "It says a lot that your dad thinks *any* kind of rapist is normal."

Sky saw Bo's faint smile and thought her friend had managed to put an end to the snide remarks. That was until Randy's brother Felix turned to face her from the row in front. He leered at her, his teeth oddly spaced like broken piano keys.

"Do you reckon the worms got to her when she was in the ground? Do you think under all them skirts they've started eating her, burrowing their way in?"

This was not normal, even for a Swiveller. Felix had been held back a year, and was, Sky suspected, an unfortunate example of the effects of inbreeding.

He had never actually spoken a word to Sky before today. Granted, he wasn't speaking directly *to* her now, but this was still an unwelcome change in behavior.

"If we open her up, will she be filled with maggots?"

Sky's chair screeched backward across the floor as she fled the classroom. She ran without thinking and soon found herself in the hallway leading to the gym. That was the last place she wanted to be, and she looked around for somewhere nobody would stare at her and imagine her insides crawling and rotten.

The janitor's closet door was usually locked, but Old Moley must have gone for a cigarette break and forgotten to shut it this time. Sky ducked inside, shutting the door, the faint tang of chemicals forcing her to breathe shallowly. It was dark in the small closet, but Sky had never been bothered by darkness. She leaned back carefully against a shelf and sighed.

"There you are."

Sean's face appeared briefly in the strip of light as he opened the door, and disappeared again as he closed it behind him. Suddenly, the small space felt ten degrees warmer, and half the size.

Something rustled, and then the space between her and Sean lit up with a white glow from his cell phone.

"It has a flashlight app," he explained. "Are you all right? Cam and Bo went to check the girls' bathrooms."

Sky nodded stiffly, very much aware that there were only a few inches separating her from Sean in the cramped space. "Yep. Fine."

"What set those creeps off like that? I don't think I've ever seen anyone upset you like that before."

A shake of Sky's head sent strands of her hair whipping against Sean's cheek. He reached up and tucked them behind her ear, and Sky forgot how to breathe.

Ask him!

Sky refused to let the Swiveller brothers and their gross ideas get in her way.

"Sean, did I . . . Did I kiss you at my birthday party?"

They were plunged into blackness as Sean dropped his phone and the light died. He cursed and they butted heads as they stooped at the same time to try and find it. Then they were both laughing, Sky clutching the sleeves of Sean's cardigan so she wouldn't topple over from her crouched position, and one of Sean's hands on her hip to help steady her. He loosened his grip once he realized where his hand was, but didn't withdraw it entirely.

"I think my butt's stuck in a mop bucket," he whispered, and they both started laughing again.

His tone grew serious again a moment later. "Why did you just ask that, about whether you kissed me?"

Sky cleared her throat. "Because I thought that I kissed you, and you were like, *WHOA*, and I kinda . . . well, I left and went down to the pier to get my head together, but then I . . ."

"Sky."

"But then I woke up in my own bed, and I knew it must have been a dream. The next day everyone said we'd just gone back inside after your fight with Randy and everyone went home early, so I really started to believe I'd dreamed it. When you hear the same thing over and over, it's like it becomes what you remember, even if you really *don't*, and I guess I don't know what to believe anymore—"

"*Sky*. You've got no idea how many times I've gone over that night, wishing it had ended differently, wishing I hadn't upset you like that. When you kissed me, I thought you felt obligated or something, because of what happened with Randy. I didn't want that to be the reason, because I knew you'd regret it and things would be weird between us. And I mean, you're *Skylar*." Sean stopped for a moment. "I went after you that night to try and explain, but it . . . but I was too late."

In truth, Sean really *did* sound as though he'd given it a lot of thought.

"Oh." Sky swallowed, and her tongue felt two sizes too big. She *had* kissed him. It hadn't been a dream at all. Her heart pounded as she realized what she needed to say if she wasn't going to spend the rest of her life wondering *what if*, like she'd been wondering for the past three months while the people she cared about thought she was rotting in the cemetery. "That wasn't why I kissed you. I kissed you because I wanted to. I've wanted to for months." *But there's probably no chance of that now, because everyone here thinks I'm some kind of zombie, and Sean's probably realized I really am a freak.*

The light went out on Sean's cell, and Sky had the impression he'd let it go out because he didn't want her to see his face.

"Good." He cleared his throat. "That's good. I just thought you were letting me down easy, after I dropped hints that could have made craters, and you acted like I had to be joking." They were close enough that she could feel the movement when he shrugged.

"Uh, no. I thought you were just goofing around." Somehow, silence in the dark stretched to several eons, and Sky scrambled for something to fill it with. "What did you mean just now, when you said I'm *Skylar*, like that's something . . . well, *something*?"

"You know how all the guys look at you, how *everyone* in this town looks at you. I think if you actually started dating me, they'd come after me with pitchforks. That doesn't mean you shouldn't, though."

He's not laughing. Normally, he'd be laughing.

Now Sky was glad he'd let the display fade out on his cell. Like all the quirks and the odd happenings of the town, the long looks were simply something she lived with. But stare at the weirdness for too long, try to fathom out the mechanics of the mystery, and the whole thing would unravel.

Maybe that's what happened to me, she thought. *They stared too long, and I unraveled.*

But she didn't want Sean to see her that way.

"It's just this town, you know. All the staring, the whispering . . . it's this Blackfin weirdness that gets into people's heads. There's nothing special about me, Sean."

"Except that you drowned, and then came back."

And what she'd believed was a dream had actually happened—
the failed kiss, her running down to the pier and taking a swan
dive off the end of it. *How* precisely she'd come to fall from the
pier was another matter, but for now Sky was left with a more
pressing question.

"Where the hell *have* I been for the last three months?"

Sean's face appeared in the glow of his cell display again.

"I don't know, Sky."

They were both quiet for a long moment in the eerie artificial light.

"What if it happens again? What if I disappear and can't find
my way back?" As much as it felt like the tendril of madness that
had wrapped around the town might tighten a little too far and
crush her, Sky knew Blackfin like she knew herself. She wouldn't,
couldn't, think of losing it. Of being lost.

Sean's hand squeezed her hip gently, reminding Sky it was still
there. "We'll have to find a way to make sure that doesn't happen."

"How can I do that when I don't understand why it's happening?" Sky said.

"By finding out exactly what made you disappear the first time,
and making sure it doesn't happen again. We'll figure it out, Sky.
I promise." He sounded so reasonable, the way he sounded when
they were working on a chemistry problem together, that it made
Sky feel better.

Sean stood abruptly, the bucket clattering on the floor behind him. He offered Sky his hands and pulled her up. Standing so close, they were almost eye to eye. Almost mouth to mouth.

Almost.

"I g-guess we should go find Cam and Bo," Sky said.

Sean opened the door for her, and she saw that he was smiling. "I guess we'd better."

❧ 6 ❧

SKY RACED OUTSIDE when the final bell rang, waving up at Silas as he spun once, urging her to keep going until her legs gave out.

She skirted past the Penny Well and ran along the main road until it split into two. Instead of taking the right fork leading up the hill to the Blood House, she went left, following the steep path down to the sea. The gravel path gave way to a dirt track through the grass, and then finally she jumped down onto the paved promenade. The sound of the sea rolling against the sand below was soothing, but the cries of the gulls overhead were sinister enough to remind Sky where she was.

It all happened how I remembered it the first time, she thought, her footsteps slowing as the pier came into view. She passed the old fortune-teller's hut at the foot of the pier and stepped out onto the old boarded platform. The wood shifted underneath her feet, but she had walked these same boards thousands of times, and would walk them a thousand more if her life kept throwing curveballs at her that required space to think big thoughts.

The wooden railing at the end of the pier reached her chest when she leaned against it. Even when the wind was high and the waves came alive, Sky found the water soothing. Catching sight of the whales and occasional dolphins that swam by was about the only draw Blackfin had for tourists, but in winter, even the most hardened whale-watchers shied away from visiting. Now that Sky thought about it, it had been some years since Blackfin had received any visitors—except the whales, of course.

No whale fins broke the surface today, though.

I tried to kiss Sean, then I came here.

Then what? She knew she hadn't jumped from the pier. She had no suicidal inclinations, and wasn't foolish enough to think of an icy swim as romantic.

But she'd been alone on the pier, hadn't she? She couldn't remember anyone else being with her. Maybe she'd tripped and fallen accidentally.

"I'm gonna take a wild guess that you're Gui's daughter."

The handrail cracked under her elbow and she jerked forward, staring at the splintered handrail turning end over end as it fell into the ocean and gripping the remaining section of the rail with white knuckles.

"Hey, careful!"

An arm wrapped around her waist. Taking a shaky breath, Sky looked over her shoulder at the guy who was holding on to her.

The first thing she noticed was his eyes—a magnetic gray that looked as deep and cold as the water she'd almost fallen into. Again.

"Jared," the guy said, the flash of metal in his tongue as he spoke proving Cam had been right about the piercing. Despite the awkward angle, Sky could see Jared was really tall, and though the arm still wrapped around her waist wasn't bulky, it was as hard as a steel cable. "Nice to meet you, Skylar."

"Jared," Sky repeated, subtly shifting until he released her. "So you're the guy working with my dad at the shop?"

"I am. But he makes me call it *le garage* when we're both there."

"That sounds like Dad. You're a mechanic, too?" Sky looked at Jared more closely. "You don't really look old enough."

"I'm nineteen," he said. "And I'm kind of a trainee. I've never worked at a garage before, but I'm a quick study and your dad doesn't mind teaching me."

"He does like to talk about his beloved *voitures*," Sky said, and Jared dipped his head in acknowledgment. "Where did you move from?"

"Oh, here and there. I moved around a lot with my grandfather growing up."

Sky almost asked where his parents were, but thought better of it. If he'd been raised by his grandfather, there really wasn't going to be a happy story behind it.

Sky saw him studying her.

"You want to know how I'm suddenly back from the dead, don't you?"

Jared shoved his hands deep into his coat pockets and pulled out a roll of mints. He held them out to her.

"I wasn't going to ask. But, of course, I'm curious. Your dad's a great guy, but for the couple of months I've worked for him, he's also been like the *most* devastated person I've ever met. I mean, *heartbroken*. And even though I just met you, I can't imagine Gui's daughter would be the kind of girl who'd just take off and leave her folks thinking she was dead. Would you like a mint?"

Sky took one from the roll and handed it back. "I didn't do it on purpose."

Jared nodded. "I figured. But it's really none of my business anyway."

They both crunched for a moment.

"How come you're not at work now?" As school let out at three, Sky knew both her parents would be working for at least a couple more hours. "Sorry, that's really none of my business."

Jared waved away her apology. "Your dad sent me home early since the shop was quiet. Figured I'd come down here and whale-watch while it's still light enough to see them."

"Me, too." Sky didn't add that she'd come down to the pier so she could spend some time on her own, trying to figure out what the hell had happened to her.

"It's a good place to come to think."

Sky wandered back to the railing, but opted not to lean against it this time.

Jared grabbed hold of the nearest section and gave it a firm yank. "It seems solid enough over here. That section must have been rotten."

But Sky wasn't really listening. She was staring at the water, seeing the sparks of light reflect from its surface, trying to remember the sensation of ice engulfing her, filling her lungs.

". . . should call someone to come down and fix it. Hey, are you all right?"

Jared touched her shoulder, and it was like being pulled back from the edge again. Sky gasped.

"Oh, uh, yeah. Sorry, spaced out for a second there. And it's Old Moley we need to call to look at the rail. The town council keeps him on retainer for this kind of thing."

Sky went to head back along the pier to the promenade, but Jared stopped her with a hand on her arm.

"You can't remember what happened to you down here that night, can you?"

Sky laughed nervously, her body tensing. "I thought you weren't going to ask me about that."

Jared let go of her and took a step back, hands up. "I'm sorry. I just thought maybe you wanted to talk about it. I didn't mean to pry."

He looked sincere. And even though he may have stood out in any normal town, with his lip ring and an electric blue streak in his dyed black hair, in Blackfin Jared was just another shade of weird. Or actually very good-looking, now that Sky thought about it. But most of all, he didn't look like he was just digging for ammunition to use against her like those dorks in homeroom.

"I remember coming here. I just can't remember anything that happened between then and when I woke up at home. And it's all gotten mixed up because everyone kept telling me over and over that it didn't happen, and after a while I just accepted that I'd dreamed it, you know?" Jared said nothing, just listened. "But leaning against the rail a moment ago, I can't see how I could accidentally fall *over* it. It's too high, and someone would have noticed if part of it had broken away like that rotten section just now."

"From what I've heard," Jared spoke softly, "it was a boy called Sean Vega who found you. He followed you down here and pulled you from the water."

"He *what?*"

He actually saw me dead? How the hell am I supposed to bring that up in conversation?

Sean was a smart guy, so he would know how to check if a person was still breathing, still had a pulse. How could he have mistakenly thought she was dead? And there must have been hospital workers, morticians, a coroner, even.

"You look like you're going to throw up."

Sky felt like it, too.

"Look, I don't know whether this will help or not, but if you really want to find out what happened that night, you might want to talk to the old gypsy." Jared nodded toward the fortune-teller's hut. "That policewoman couldn't find her to question her when it happened, but I found out where she went after leaving the hut. And I figure if she left in such a hurry, it was because she saw what went down, and it scared her. Now that doesn't sound like she just saw you fall, does it?"

Sky's fingernails dug grooves in her palms. "How do you know all this?"

"It was all anyone could talk about when I arrived in Blackfin," Jared said. "And some I figured out when I spotted an old woman walking stark naked near the old church in the woods."

"There's a church in the woods?" Sky found herself stepping closer to Jared once more. "Nobody goes into Blackfin Woods."

"I did. And the old woman does, too. I'm assuming she must be the gypsy who disappeared from the hut. Unless you know of some other old lady who'd be living in a ruined church?"

Sky shook her head. Madame Curio was well known in Blackfin, even though she was avoided by most.

"How did you even get in there?" The woods had been secured against intruders for as long as Sky could remember, the talk of roaming wolves and lightning-trees that electrocuted passing children not being enough to keep out idle teenagers.

"I have my ways. I could go with you to talk to her, if you like? You want to find out what happened to you, don't you?"

One second turned into several, and Sky realized she'd been staring at him.

"I should really be heading home. I have to go."

"Don't you want answers, Sky? Hey, where are you going?"

Sky ran down the length of the pier, not pausing as she passed the fortune-teller's hut with its gaping, empty windows.

She kept going along the promenade and up the hill, until she had to either stop or risk throwing up in her own front yard. But as the Blood House came into view, she knew she didn't want to be there on her own, either. As much as she loved her house, she couldn't face pretending not to see the strange things she always saw there, the whispers and creaks and shifting wood grain that sometimes, *sometimes*, resembled a face.

She didn't want to deal with anything mysterious for just a little while. So instead, she headed for Gui's garage.

"Hi, *coco*." Gui slid out from beneath the car he was working on. "What on earth is the matter?"

Gui wiped his oil-blackened hands on a rag before guiding his daughter to sit on one of the workbenches. Sky debated whether or not she should tell him about all the craziness—the old fortune-teller living in the woods, Jared's weird interest in what had happened to her, what Bo had said about someone digging up her grave. But at the same time, she felt almost certain her parents were keeping things from her. They'd been tiptoeing around her like she was terminally ill, whispering behind closed doors and trying to keep her from talking to Officer Vega.

And despite her mother's maidenly wilting on the day she had supposedly *reappeared*, they weren't exactly acting like a couple whose daughter had miraculously returned from the dead. In fact, they were doing everything they could to act as though nothing at all had happened.

Maybe Officer Vega was right, and I should ask Mom about what happened that night. Confront her, maybe.

But Sky knew she'd have no luck tackling her mother head-on. If Lily Rousseau wanted to keep something a secret, it stayed a secret.

The unanswered questions remained a cold, hard wall between Sky and her parents, and it meant that telling her dad what was happening in the hopes he'd fill in the blanks was only going to leave her feeling hurt and disappointed. Fighting with her dad was about the last thing Sky could deal with right now.

"Nothing, don't worry. Just had a crappy day is all."

Sky closed her eyes as her father kissed her forehead. "I don't have any hot chocolate, but I can easily go to get some if it will make you feel better."

Gui's solution to most problems was hot chocolate, which Sky would have found ridiculous if she didn't also admit that it worked. Most of the time.

"No, I'm good. It looks like you have work to do, and I just kinda wanted to come and sit for a while, if that's okay."

Gui disappeared into his office at the back of the shop for a second and came back with his old sheepskin coat. He wrapped it around Sky, and nodded in satisfaction.

"Sit as long as you like, *coco*. But it gets drafty *dans le garage*, and your mother will strike me down if I let you catch a chill."

They both burst out laughing at the unlikely image. She might loose the occasional string of expletives into the ether, but Lily would never raise a hand against her supersized husband.

"Thanks, Dad," Sky said softly, then watched her father get back to work on the new Chrysler, which she recognized as belonging to Miss Schwarz, her science teacher.

Before long Sky felt her head sinking toward the metal workbench, and Gui's arms gathering her up.

"Time to go home, I think." He chuckled, and Sky let herself drift off to sleep while her dad buckled her into the cab of his truck.

⚜

IT WAS NOT the broken whispers drifting from her parents' room that woke Sky, but the shifting groans of the old house. It was as though the Blood House was carefully coaxing her from sleep to listen.

"You knew she . . . like him, Lily."

"But I never knew Severin . . . his gift was . . . How was I to know?"

She rolled to face the wall, fully expecting the grain of the wooden paneling to have shifted with the shadows. The Blood House did not disappoint her.

The friendly face of an old man held a finger to his lips, there and yet not when she concentrated on the texture of the wood. Nevertheless, Sky listened.

". . . knew she would . . . never asked Severin . . . the circus burned . . ."

Unable to make sense of the snatches drifting through the old walls, Sky crept from her room, keeping to the edges of the floorboards to minimize the creaks. But it seemed the Blood House wanted her to hear, its boards making no sound as she carefully leaned against the door to her parents' bedroom.

"I thought we had left all of this behind the night of the fire."

Sky's father moved across the room toward the wardrobe, the sound of the floorboards giving him away.

"The woods can't hold our secrets forever," Lily said, "no matter how hard we try to keep them hidden. But how can we make Sky . . . How can we help her understand, Gui, if we don't know how it works ourselves? Severin only told me bits and pieces, and I could never tell when he was being truthful."

The woods again? First Jared, now my parents.

Gui made a deep noise of agreement in his throat. "I wonder why she doesn't seem to know she left, and yet she is aware that three months have passed since that night. It's just . . . *c'est de la folie.*"

Lily made no audible response, though Sky pressed her ear more tightly to the door to try to discern her movements. When a few seconds had passed and she still heard nothing, Sky suspected her mother's light-footedness was about to expose her in the act of spying. So she crept away, back to her room.

❧ 7 ❧

BLACKFIN WOODS WAS a forbidding place. The locals spoke of three great silver wolves being sighted beyond the boundary, but Sky didn't believe those rumors. The truth was no doubt something far more probable—like the town council meeting there to hold séances under the full moon, or Old Moley using the woods to grow those sweet-smelling mushrooms he ground into his pipe when he thought nobody was looking.

Sky's footsteps cast echoes through the night, the spiked silhouettes of the treetops looming ahead of her.

She wrapped her coat more tightly around herself, though the night wasn't quite cold enough to leave frost on the ground. But being alone at midnight at the woods' edge carried its own icy coldness, and Sky felt it.

As she rounded the last twist of road, Sky caught the glint of light on metal. It wasn't the black coils of the iron gate or the knifepoint tips topping the fence, but the brand new, well-oiled chain that barred all from entering.

She strode up to the iron gates, craning her neck to assess their height and the likelihood of being able to scale them unscathed. Many stories—no doubt exaggerated by cunning parents—had filtered down to Sky's ears about kids who had attempted the climb, only to reach the point of no return and find the lack of footholds led to inevitable impalement. She looked down at her boots. They weren't as ridiculous for climbing as sandals or clogs would have been, but the black twists of iron looked awfully slippery.

"Maybe not," she said, wishing Jared had told her how he had gotten inside the fence.

Sky's breath misted in front of her. She searched the darkness in both directions, looking for any obvious weak spots in the fence. None presented themselves, but that didn't mean they weren't there. Going on instinct alone, Sky followed the stretch of iron railings leading off to her right. Allowing her left hand to trail along the cold metal, Sky began counting her footsteps in the dark.

"Twenty-eight, twenty-nine . . ."

The fence curved around, setting the woods in this section back a little farther from the road. No streetlamps lit the secluded stretch of pavement, so moving away from it was like stepping into an abyss. The trees seemed to lean forward in anticipation as Sky moved along, and she shrank away from them, no longer certain that the lightning-trees were a myth.

"Eighty-two, eighty-three . . ."

Soon the fence cut in farther from the road, skinny crabapple trees crowding in from both sides. Barren branches like children's finger bones pointed down at Sky. With the toe of her boot, she kicked up a pile of leaves at the nearest tree, glad that nobody was watching her for a change. But they hadn't been watching her for months if they all believed she was dead, buried underneath the clay soil to be eaten by worms.

"One hundred thirty, one hundred thirty-one—"

A flash of lightning split the sky, showing her the battered teeth of gravestones pegged into the meadow before her. The forks of light seemed to swirl around her, but just for a moment.

Sky spun in a circle, looking for the iron fence her hand had rested on moments ago, but she couldn't see it anywhere.

She was lost.

Sky stopped short. That couldn't be right. She *never* got lost in Blackfin.

Except when you go missing for three months and everyone thinks you're dead, she answered herself with a snort.

Lightning flashed again, almost close enough to touch this time, and with that same viscous quality.

Dizziness swept over her. She hadn't been hit with a migraine this bad in months.

The nausea was sudden and intense, and Sky braced her hands on her knees until it passed. When she looked up, she met the crooked grin of Blackfin Cemetery.

How the hell have I ended up here? The cemetery's half a mile from the woods!

As her eyes cleared, Sky saw the mounded grave in front of her. Her own name mocked her in bold letters across the headstone, with her birth and death dates below—exactly sixteen years apart. But despite Bo's assertion, the grave was undisturbed.

Strange images appeared in the strands of light weaving around her—places and things she shouldn't, *couldn't*, be seeing—and Sky clenched her eyes shut.

It didn't help.

She tripped and landed on her backside as she scrambled away from her own grave.

"I'm not dead," Sky whispered, then repeated it. Over and over again she spoke her mantra, even as she ran toward the cemetery gates. Her shaky breathing turned to sobs.

Lightning scored her peripheral vision, chasing her, taunting her, until she was suddenly—inexplicably—on her own front porch.

No way I ran that quickly, she thought, still gasping on tears and stolen breath. *It's not possible.*

Yet the evidence was as tangible as the painted green door now swinging open to usher her inside the Blood House.

8

THE TWO ELDEST Swiveller brothers stared at Sky as she walked into homeroom the next day, then turned away. Their well of witty comments had run dry already. Sky tried to emulate her mother's perfect posture as she held her head up and shoulders back, took off her coat, and draped it over the back of the chair next to Bo.

"Where's Cam today?"

Bo looked up from the magazine she'd been reading. "She had to visit the orthodontist in Oakridge this morning. She should be here after lunch, though."

Sky swallowed her disappointment. She had no classes with Cam after lunch, and she'd wanted to ask both her friends to come with her to talk to the old woman in the woods. After stumbling across her own grave in Blackfin Cemetery, Sky was a little gun-shy about making another attempt to break in by herself.

"How come you said my grave's been dug up? I saw it yesterday, and it doesn't look like anyone's messed with it."

Bo shrugged. "It was definitely messed with when I was there on Friday. Maybe you were at the wrong grave."

"But it had my name on the headstone!"

Bo closed her magazine. "What do you want me to say? It

was a big, empty hole last time I saw it. If someone filled it back in, or moved your headstone to another grave or something, I know nothing about it."

Sky sat back, knowing this was getting her nowhere, and that Bo would just ignore her altogether if she kept badgering her. "Are you busy later? Tonight, I mean?"

"Yup. Mom's off to visit the old man, so I'm stuck babysitting the howlers."

Bo's six-year-old twin brothers had truly earned their nickname. Even when perfectly content, they made enough noise to warrant earplugs and had a seemingly endless supply of energy to climb furniture and swing from drapes. With Bo's general listlessness, it was amazing that they were even related.

Sky tried to come up with another plan while Mr. Hiatt took the roll. Though he still looked like he might bolt at any minute, he at least managed to talk to her without having a seizure.

Sky was left alone throughout her morning classes, and had even started to relax by lunchtime.

Then the whispers started.

"What's going on?" Sky set her lunch tray down opposite Bo.

Bo spoke without looking up from her phone. "Cam's aunt showed up earlier. She found your coffin—you know, from the grave you said *hadn't* been disturbed—in the Swivellers' barn. When they opened it, all they found inside was the Swivellers' dead dog,

Clarence, dressed in your clothes. Officer Vega thinks they must have dug it up not long after you returned from the dead, so she's taken all four of them in for questioning."

"Bo, I *wasn't* dead."

"You were."

Sky ignored her.

"Do you think they actually found a body in there when they first opened it?" Bo asked, appearing more curious than disturbed by the possibility.

"Do you think it was really them? Could the Swivellers have dug up my grave?"

Bo picked at her egg salad. "Of course it was them."

"But *why?*"

Bo put down her fork, finally looking up at Sky with narrowed eyes. "Because they're bobble-headed weirdos who have nothing better to do than sneak around digging up corpses that aren't there and filling their clothes with dead dogs." Bo poked her egg salad again and grimaced. "How old do you think this shit is?"

Sky leaned over to examine it. "It sure looks deader than I do."

❧❦❧

Cam, can you sneak out with me 18r? Need to talk to M Curio, heard she's camping nr old church in woods. Wear climbing shoes. X

Sky hit SEND, then sat back against her headboard and waited. She'd gone up to her room early, claiming she was catching up on the homework she'd missed. That was another rotten thing about her situation—all the homework she'd done over the last three months had vanished along with that separate life she had been living. So now she rescrawled her schoolwork by flashlight under her sheets while she waited until it was safe to sneak out.

But when half an hour had passed without a response from Cam, Sky began to get restless.

Cam??

Another half hour passed, and Sky heard her parents go to bed. Ten minutes later, the faint sound of her mother's snoring told her at least one of them was sleeping. She had come close to backing out when her mother, thinking Sky was asleep, had crept in and leaned to kiss her gently on the forehead. But Sky needed to do this.

The house creaked, a weary stretch of its bones, before it settled for the night. It was time to leave, but Sky could admit that she was frightened by the prospect of confronting crazy old Madame Curio by herself.

Heading over to your place now in case you haven't got credit to reply or whatever.

Sky laced up her flat-soled boots, put on her long coat and leather gloves—leather being the best option for scaling spike-tipped fences—and checked she had everything she might need in her book bag. Which was really just the heavy-duty flashlight she'd been using to do her homework.

Sky opened the french windows and slid over the rail before dropping nimbly into her father's vegetable patch. She kicked and scuffed the soil a little so her parents would think the mess had been made by stray cats fighting again, and jogged away from the house as quietly as possible.

Sky moved quickly past the houses lining her street, searching for movement in every shadow.

The Vega household lay in darkness when Sky reached the driveway. Keeping to the shadows underneath the twisted willow, Sky crept toward the house with her eyes fixed on Cam's upstairs window and her mind focused on figuring out how she could alert her friend to her presence without also waking the police officer in the next bedroom.

"*Sky.*"

Sky jumped like a cat at Sean's urgent whisper. Peering through the shadows she could just about make him out through the open window of his Jeep.

"*Get in.*"

Sky tiptoed to the passenger side and climbed in with as much grace as she could muster after being caught skulking around his front yard. They both winced as her door closed with a *snick*.

"Sean, what are you doing here?"

He held a finger to his lips and put the car in neutral, coasting it slowly down the slope of the driveway and halfway along Provencher Street before pulling over and starting the car's engine.

"Cam had her braces tightened earlier and it gave her a migraine. I heard your messages come through on her phone downstairs, so I checked them in case it was anything urgent. Lucky I did," he added, smiling. "Aunt Holly was getting curious about the beeps."

"Thanks," Sky said, reaching for the door handle. "And I'm sorry you had to sneak around . . ."

"Where are you going?"

"I am going to go home."

Even in the dark Sky saw the exasperated look on his face. "If you want to go home, I'll drive you there. But you said you needed to speak to Madame Curio. Does this have something to do with figuring out what happened to you?"

Sky nodded.

"You could have asked me to go with you, you know. I *want* to help you figure this out." He grinned at her again. "I'm even wearing my climbing shoes."

Sky laughed as he tried to maneuver one leg from beneath the steering wheel to show her and accidentally flipped on his headlights.

"I really don't need you to . . ." A flicker of hurt crossed Sean's face, and Sky reeled in her words. ". . . show off your superfly footwear, Sean." He snickered, and Sky couldn't help grinning back at him. "I guess we're going to the woods."

❦

ICE CRYSTALS SPARKLED in the grass as Sky led the way.

"Isn't your coat going to get in the way?" Sean's voice was unnaturally loud in the absolute silence of the woods. They hadn't yet reached the fence where Sky had somehow lost her bearings on her previous visit, but the crabapple trees were beckoning not far ahead.

"It was this coat or no coat," she answered. "My mom is kind of strict about what I wear, so she only lets me keep what she approves of."

"How come?"

"I don't know," Sky said. "She'll just donate anything of mine she doesn't like to Goodwill. One time, when I went down to the thrift store and bought back a pair of jeans I loved, she washed them in bleach. They were totally ruined." Sky reached up and wrapped her hand around one of the iron railings. "We're here."

Sean looked up at the iron spikes on top of the fence. "*This* is what you were planning to climb over?" He shook his head, unzipping his duffle coat and pulling out a metal jack. "Seriously."

Sky watched as he used the jack—the same type as the ones she'd seen lying around her dad's garage—to widen the gap between two of the railings. He kept winding it until the space was just big enough for them to fit through.

"You just happened to have a car jack hidden in your jacket?"

"You mean you don't?" Sean looked up, his teeth visible in the moonlight as he grinned. "When you said we were going to the woods, I figured what you had in mind. Bringing the jack from the trunk of my car seemed like the best way to make sure neither of us gets impaled."

Sean squeezed through the gap he'd made and reached back to take Sky's hand. Sky followed Sean through, grabbing her skirt with her free hand to avoid tripping over it.

They walked into Blackfin Woods, the trees becoming denser and denser around them.

"Hang on a sec." Sky tugged on Sean's hand, realizing for the first time that he hadn't released it after she'd squeezed through the fence, and fished her flashlight from her book bag. A narrow beam sliced outward when she switched it on, dark shapes shuffling away into the shadows.

Sky let her free hand drop back down to her side, cold inside her leather glove without Sean's to warm it. Even in the middle of the woods, with creatures scuttling around their feet and in almost total darkness, Sky had to fight to keep from smiling as his fingers wrapped around hers again a moment later. It felt natural, as though his hand had been made to fit hers.

"How do you know we're going the right way?" Sky whispered, and he pointed upward through the high branches. "You're following the stars?"

"Uh, no. I'm following the church spire. You said she was near the church, right?"

And then Sky saw it, blacker than the sky. The church spire leaned awkwardly, but Sky could still make out the shape of the bell at the top of the tower.

Well, that's one mystery solved, she thought. The discovery of where the hourly chime originated seemed like a good omen. Maybe she would find answers to her own mystery in the woods.

"What if Madame Curio's not here?" Sky whispered. They both knew that she was really asking, *What if she is here?*

"Then we come back again. And again. Until we manage to find her and get some answers."

He sounded so certain that Sky had no choice but to believe him. Then she spotted something up ahead, paler than the shadows surrounding it.

"Is that a van?" Sky whispered, shutting off the flashlight on instinct.

"I can't see now."

"Sorry." She panned the light.

It was indeed a VW van.

"I don't recognize it," Sean whispered back, "and if anyone's inside, it doesn't look like they're awake."

They walked over to it and peered in through the windows. Nothing moved in the shadowy interior, so Sky shined the light through the windows. Inside, the van was a mess of old junk and clothes strewn about, but it was hard to say whether someone had been living in it recently.

She killed the light again. "Maybe it's abandoned. I'm not even sure how someone could drive it here in the first place, with the fence surrounding the woods. Come on, we're almost at the church. Maybe that's where she's camping out."

They moved more slowly now, keeping the flashlight off in case Madame Curio could see them coming.

Only two walls of the church remained mostly intact—the rest appeared to have been destroyed by fire. The rear corner of the stone building had been struck by a tree, perhaps felled in an attempt to contain the flames from spreading farther. It hadn't worked. The charred carcasses of trees stood out farther back in the silvery light, blacker than black, their gnarled branches too barren even for winter.

It was difficult to tell whether anything moved from within the church, the angle of the moonlight creating planes and angles that didn't belong to the ruins. Only the precarious spire was easily identified, looking like a giant's hammer waiting to fall.

They crept around the side of the church, careful not to walk where the spire might strike if it chose that moment to crash down. Suddenly, Sean stopped, his fingers squeezing Sky's gloved hand.

She couldn't tell what he'd seen. He wasn't looking inside the church, but deeper into the woods.

Sky clicked on the light, and it shone directly on a naked old woman standing in front of them.

❦ 9 ❦

"**AREN'T YOU COLD,** Madame Curio?"

The old woman disappeared as soon as Sky spoke, and Sky had to pan the flashlight quickly to find her standing not more than three feet away from them, now wrapped in a toga fashioned from a plaid blanket.

"Old bones are always cold. Are your bones still cold after being in the water, child? But they never were, were they? Not in the water, not in the ground. Not these ones, leastways." She poked Sky's shoulder with a clawlike finger, and Sky edged a little closer to Sean.

Madame Curio shuffled off in her blanket toga as though she hadn't moved like a whip moments earlier. They followed her past the crumbling edge of the church's south wall and saw that she had made a shelter out of old tarpaulins. The massive fallen oak lay diagonally through the building, and Madame Curio was watching them from her perch at the far end of it.

"See how you cling to each other. Like two magnets pulling together, isn't it?" Sky looked down at their intertwined hands self-consciously, but neither of them pulled away. "Better than being set adrift, I suppose." The old woman didn't seem entirely convinced. "But you came for answers, and I only have time for one. Ask a question."

Sky was stuck for words for a few moments before she remembered why they had come.

"What happened to me the night I disappeared?"

The old woman's eyes sparked like two flints. "Be specific, child. You have disappeared more than once, and will again."

Sky had no idea what the old woman meant by that, but she persevered. "What happened to me at the pier on my birthday?"

The old woman smiled. "Better question would be *who*, not *what*, but never mind. You were chased, and you jumped off the pier."

"I *jumped*?"

Madame Curio nodded. "You had little choice. But that's two questions, and you have stolen my time."

"Wait, chased? By who?"

But even as Sky took a tentative step toward the old woman, the clock began to strike in the tower above them, and a low rumbling sounded through the trees all around.

"You have brought him here, damn you! Severin would be so angry with me." Madame Curio leaped to her feet, squinting through one of the broken windows into the heart of the woods. Underneath the sill, a tarnished plaque bearing the name REVEREND SILAS PEALE with some indecipherable lettering underneath, swung like a pendulum from its single remaining screw.

The low roar that had startled Madame Curio was building, getting closer as the clock continued to count the hours.

Ten, eleven, twelve.

Sky shivered. Something about that sound, that low growl all around her, getting closer by the second . . .

"Come on!" Sean tugged on her hand, urging her to run with him, back the way they had come.

"What about Madame Curio?" Sky looked around for the old woman, but she had vanished again.

"She climbed up into the spire. Whoever's driving that van, she seemed awfully anxious not to talk to them, so I'm thinking we need to get out of here."

The van. Sky realized what the growling noise really was— the engine of the old van they'd seen on their way to the church, echoing through the clearing. Whoever the van belonged to, they'd obviously returned.

Sky scrambled over the rough ground, trying to hold her skirt up with one hand and hold on to Sean with the other until they were deep into the thick of the trees again. Sean stopped, catching Sky as she nearly tripped, and pulled her into the shadows. A beam of light sliced into the dark toward them. Once, twice, it passed near to where they stood breathing hard, and disappeared as the flashlight's owner moved on.

Sky sank against Sean's chest. "Who *was* that?"

She looked up to find Sean's eyes fixed on her. Her fingers had clenched around the fabric of his duffle coat when they had ducked behind the tree, and now his hands covered hers. Sky wondered when exactly she had taken off her gloves.

"We should head back to the fence," Sky whispered into the air between them.

"We should," Sean agreed, but didn't move. His eyes dipped to her mouth for a moment, and he swallowed.

Sky looked around for signs of the way they'd come into the woods. There were no tracks that she could make out, and the more she looked at the dense trees surrounding them, the more lost she felt.

"I'm not sure which way we came in, but if we keep going in a straight line, we'll reach the fence eventually," Sky said.

Sean held out his hand, like it had become a normal thing for them to always be touching. "Let's go."

⚜

STURDY OAKS GAVE way to spindly saplings, and the ground crunched beneath their feet as Sky and Sean picked their way through the woods.

"Do you know you hum when you're thinking?"

Sky looked up from watching for obstacles in her path and stopped. "I do?"

Sean smiled. "You do it in study hall, too. Especially when we're studying physics."

She groaned.

"I think it's really cute. I've missed hearing it."

Sky stopped breathing, but Sean had already started walking again. Now that she was looking up and not at her feet, though, she saw something that made her blood run cold.

"Sean."

He stopped and peered off into the darkness where her eyes were fixed. There, against an ink-black sky, twisted metal poles flew rags for flags, some with the tattered remains of the tent still attached to the circular frames.

"What is that?"

There was no reason for Sky to know what it was, but she had never been more certain of anything. "It's a circus."

"Why would there be a circus in the middle of the woods?"

Sky didn't answer. She was staring at the skeletal frames, feeling that some strange darkness beyond the wintry night had settled over the debris, almost hearing the sounds of the ringmaster calling in the acts to perform, the families cheering and gasping at the spectacles before them. . . .

"Sky?"

Lightning split the sky overhead, and in the flash Sky saw the tents as they had been—the candy-striped Big Top surrounded by smaller tents, people milling among them with all the garish lights and sounds of the circus drawing them in. . . .

"SKYLAR!"

Sean's arms wrapped around her like he was afraid she'd run, but she had snapped out of her daydream.

"Thank God, I thought . . . Please don't disappear again. I have no idea what just happened, but you started to . . . fade," Sean said.

"Fade?" Sky felt an icy chill on her skin. "Please take me home, Sean."

They hurried on through the woods, neither stopping nor talking until the fence faced them and they were able to follow it to the gap where they had come in. It was all Sky could do to keep her eyes open on the short ride home, but Sean kept shooting worried glances her way every few seconds.

"I'm not going anywhere," she said, but whether to Sean or herself she wasn't sure.

❖ 10 ❖

SKY COULD HAVE slept for days. So it was with some resentment that she grumbled and cursed her way to school the next morning.

"How's your head?"

Cam's response was to groan and whap her forehead against the desk.

"I hate my braces. They are the devil's train tracks."

"Shoulda got them out of the way sooner," Bo answered. "Like I did." Then she smiled in a way that was completely un-Bo-like, showing off her perfectly straight, white teeth.

"Margaret Peeps?"

Bo's grin turned sour at the use of her real name, and vanished completely as her eyes fell on Principal Hemlock in the doorway. All three girls knew what this meant: Bo's father had been released again. Mrs. Peeps always pulled Bo and her brothers out of school when her dad was coming home from his latest stint in jail, and Sky knew what her friend was about to ask even before she hissed, "I need to stay over at your house tonight. If my mom asks, we're having a study sleepover." She looked from Sky to Cam until they both nodded, then followed Principal Hemlock out of the room.

Cam turned to Sky with a grin until her jaw clenched in pain. "Yay, thleepover!"

⚜

THOUGH, SCIENTIFICALLY SPEAKING, there should have been a finite number of marshmallows Guillaume Rousseau could fit into each mug of hot chocolate, he managed to far exceed this number for the occasion of the girls' impromptu sleepover.

Bo took a sip, looking reluctantly comfortable in her pink bunny pajamas and wearing a hot-foam moustache.

"How's your dad doing?" Sky asked, fully anticipating the eye-roll Bo shot at her.

"Jeez, if we're gonna talk about that loser we might as well actually do homework."

"But I know what we *could* talk about," Cam piped up, looking far too bubbly for someone with an alleged migraine. "Where you and Sean went sneaking off to so late last night." Then her eyes widened. "Unless it's something I really don't want to know."

Sky groaned and let her head fall back against her headboard. "It was nothing like that. I told you I was going to talk to Madame Curio, to see if she saw anything from her hut that night." At Cam's blank look, Sky realized Sean must have deleted the messages from Cam's phone in case their aunt's curiosity got the better of her. "Sean's just helping me try to figure out what happened the night of my party."

Bo snorted. "What is there to figure out, really?" Both Cam and Sky stared at her. "I mean, do you seriously think you're going to be able to just figure out how you *died* and suddenly showed up three months later? Like you'll realize the wrong page was showing on the calendar or some dumb thing, and it'll all be neatly explained away?" The two other girls said nothing. "Exactly. This is some weird Blackfin shit you've gotten yourself into, and you're never going to figure out the why and the how because there *is* no why or how."

"I'll help you figure it out," Cam whispered. "And Sean's good at solving problems."

"Pfeh!" Bo scowled into her hot chocolate.

Sky wondered how these two had remained friends for the last three months without her as a buffer.

"Thanks, Cam, but to be honest I'm not sure where to go from here. I'm at a bit of a dead end, information-wise."

And things just keep getting weirder and weirder the more I dig for answers.

Their conversation turned to more normal things until Sky's mom popped her head around the door and made it clear the noise was to cease immediately. For once, Sky was grateful. The tiredness she'd been feeling on and off all week had returned like a twenty-pound cat sitting on her head. She tuned out Cam's occasional whispers asking if she was still awake, Bo's gentle snores from across the room, and the shifting grains of the woodwork, which seemed to be pointing toward the french windows.

Sky smiled and drew the covers more tightly around her. This was her life, her home.

⚜

THE SOUND OF bells was growing louder and louder.

Sky blinked, and lights flashed, but she couldn't imagine why they were still visible when she closed her eyes. Something cold and wet dripped onto her shoulder, and she looked up to find a trickle of orange liquid escaping through some kind of slats above her head.

Sky pushed herself up, wiping what felt like sawdust from the heels of her hands onto her pajama bottoms. The air around her was sickly sweet, almost too thick to breathe.

"We need to kill him! It's the only way we'll ever be free."

The voice was whispering, but the urgent tone allowed it to carry over the loud music she not only heard, but felt throbbing in the ground beneath her. Sky tried to angle her neck to see who could have spoken, but the bleachers hid all but a faint strip of light and footwear from her.

"You know that's impossible. At least until I've got the skull back."

This second voice was definitely a man's, and somewhere nearby. Sky's feet were bare, so she picked her way carefully between metal posts and garbage, toward where she thought the voices had come from. When she reached the end of the grandstand, Sky had to crawl to get out from under the pitched seating. She crept along the striped tarpaulin covering the tent, where she was less visible.

Because Sky was definitely inside a tent. A huge, round affair with its topmost peak at least fifty feet in the air. She watched as a colossus with rippling muscles plucked several large hatchets from a man-size corkboard. It looked like his act was over, and a group of bedraggled children heaved the lengths of chain the colossus had been using out of the arena. He stalked out after them, his back to the audience and massive shoulders hunching when the crowd applauded.

The band finished their song as the next act entered the ring—two painfully thin women in sparkling leotards carrying swords of various shapes and sizes. With the band no longer playing, Sky heard voices coming from behind the tarpaulin at her back. She felt along the fabric until she found the edge and made a crack—small enough to peer through without being seen herself.

"Listen, lady, I paid good money for you to find my daughter!"

A man was standing not far from where Sky stood spying, his arm wrapped around a sobbing woman as they huddled with a third person. Even in the flickering light from the carnival attractions outside the Big Top, Sky recognized the third person as her mother. Her hair was much longer and ironed straight, and she looked younger, somehow, despite the worry drawing her lips into a tight line. But it was definitely Lily Rousseau, and she appeared to be getting both barrels from the man facing her. The other woman—his wife, Sky guessed—leaned against him, her shoulders trembling.

"I did explain that I'd only be able to tell you what happened to her around the time she was taken. She left with a couple who looked a lot like you, and she wasn't scared of them. That's all I see."

Sky wondered what her mother could possibly be talking about. She wondered, too, if she should walk out and speak to her mother, but a hand like a mace fell on Sky's shoulder, and she looked up into her father's face. He, too, seemed to have under-gone some antiaging miracle, the laugh lines around his eyes and mouth looking far less pronounced than usual, his normally bald head covered in a thick mat of red hair.

This has got to be some freaky-ass dream.

"Excuse me, young lady, but I need to get past you."

Not a single flicker of recognition passed through his eyes, though he did look a little perplexed when his eyes fell to her pajamas. Looking at his billowing silk pants and satin waistcoat, Sky realized this was the man she had just seen pulling hatchets from a corkboard.

Gui made his way past her as she stared, inserting himself between her mother and the other couple. But whatever had upset the husband was too powerful to be subdued by Gui's imposing presence.

"I will have the police down here so fast—"

Gui raised one hand, silencing him instantly. "I would strongly suggest you do not, monsieur. My friend has done as she promised, with fair warning that she might not see where your child is now. You have my sympathy, but there is nothing more to be done."

The man sputtered a protest, but eventually the couple left, leaving Sky's parents alone outside the tent.

"You must not see these people alone anymore, Lily. Not in your condition."

"Our next act will mesmerize and entrance, fascinate and perplex! Watch our amazing mind-and-body-bending double-act—Contortia and Mole Man!"

The music started up again, the band and bells mingling together, sinking under her skin until they felt like a part of her. It was terrifying and irresistible at the same time, a voice without words calling her back inside.

Sky ducked under the hanging tarpaulin and saw the ring-master staring straight at her from across the Big Top. He wore his blond hair slicked back beneath a top hat, which somehow didn't look ridiculous. His tailored red coat was fastened with brass buttons, shining like they had been freshly polished. He dipped his head, the gesture somewhere between confusion and acknowledgment.

Something about this man drew Sky in the same way the circus had called to her.

This is crazy. It's a dream, that's all. A freaky, messed-up dream.

Sky pinched herself on the arm, waiting for the scene to fade around her, but nothing happened. The ringmaster frowned as he watched her, like he'd forgotten about the hundreds of people watching him at the center of the circle.

Who are you? he mouthed as the contortionist flounced past him in her purple sequins and began stuffing herself into a lockbox so that her partner could seal her inside.

The ringmaster stepped out of the spotlight and began circling the arena at the center of the Big Top, not once taking his eyes from her. Something about the look in his eyes had Sky scrabbling for the edge of the tent flap.

I want to wake up now. I want to go home!

She darted out from under it, narrowly avoiding running into a young family whose children were sticky with cotton candy. Sky ducked around them, sparing a glance behind her in case the man was following. But when she turned it wasn't the ringmaster she saw, or even the Big Top. A ghastly white face stared at her from the darkness beyond the tent, eyes boring into her greedily. Sky screamed as lightning flashed all around her, blinding her.

I want to go home!

When her eyes cleared, the face had vanished, and the only light Sky saw was the flickering of the TV coming from the family room. Everything was quiet, safe. Sky could tell she was in her own home once more. In the kitchen. In her pajamas.

The sweetness of the relief she felt was followed by a sinking realization: *I'm officially losing it.*

A quick glance around the corner showed her father asleep on the sofa, a late-night reality TV show on mute. Careful not to wake him, Sky crept in to grab the old throw hanging over the back of the sofa and draped it over him. She leaned over to switch off the TV with the remote, and froze. In the square of light reflected on the darkened TV screen, a dark outline appeared behind her. Sky whirled, accidentally kicking the corner of the sofa. Her father grunted in his sleep.

There was nobody there.

Only the large picture window stood behind her, the shadows of the garden absent of any sign of someone having recently disturbed them. Sky stood for a minute, watching, willing her heart to stop kicking her ribs. Still nothing moved outside the window.

Dad, wake up!

But Gui continued to sleep soundly on the sofa, and Sky

refused to wake him because she'd been frightened by . . . what?

Finally deciding that she'd lost her mind and there was nothing more to be done about it, Sky went back upstairs to her room, tiptoed past her sleeping friends, and got back into her bed.

Sky stared at her ceiling, dead tired but too scared to sleep. She knew it hadn't really been a dream—the still-drying patch of orange soda sticking her cami top to her proved as much. The circus had burned to the ground, she had seen its charred shell in the woods with Sean. So there was no way she had simply sleep-walked back there, either.

And if the itching was anything to go by, Sky would have some explaining to do when Lily discovered the sawdust in Sky's pajama pants.

11

THE MOVEMENT OF Miss Schwarz's red fingernails was hypnotic as she wrote out equations on the board. Sky's eyes wandered in and out of focus, making the lines blur.

"Now make sure you copy this down, because—hint, hint—it may just be on your midterm."

Sky picked up her pencil, her head spinning. Even the hard surface of the desk looked so tempting. If she could just rest her eyes for a moment, she'd feel much better.

No, no, no! I don't want to go back; I don't want to be lost again. . . .

"Where did you go, Skylar Rousseau?"

Sky jerked her head up off the table to find the whole class, including Miss Schwarz, staring at her. Miss Schwarz leaned in across Sky's desk and lowered her voice.

"Tell me. Where did you go? I need to know!" Miss Schwarz's words had become a hiss, her face twisted so that she looked much older than her forty-or-so years. Sky edged away.

"I'm not sure what you mean, Miss Schwarz."

"I think you should stay after class so we can talk about—"

"Miss Schwarz, can't you see she's not feeling well?"

Sky jumped. Sean had been sitting in the far corner across

the room a moment ago, but now he was standing behind her, almost protectively.

Sky ducked her head, her cheeks flushed.

"I really think you should—"

"Of course, I'll take Sky to the nurse's office, if you insist."

Sean deftly grabbed Sky's books and her bag, and steered her out of class before Miss Schwarz could do anything more than stutter. Outside in the hallway, Sky snatched her bag from Sean's hands.

"What the hell was that?"

"Sorry." He didn't look at all sorry. "You just looked like you needed to get out of there. I'm learning to recognize your *flight risk* expression." Sean's mouth pinched at the corners like he'd meant to smile, but it didn't quite manifest.

"You mean like when I ran from you the night I . . . the night of my birthday?" Sky's heart knocked against her ribs as Sean's eyes fixed on hers.

"I was only minutes—*minutes*—behind you, Sky. But by the time I got to the pier, you'd already . . ."

"But you came after me."

Sean shoved his hands in his pockets and looked down at his sneakers. "Of course I came after you. It was my stupid fault you were upset."

Sky reached out and put a hand on his arm, hoping he would look at her like he'd looked at her two nights ago in the woods.

When she'd thought he was about to kiss her.

"Do you actually need to go to the nurse's office?"

His question caught Sky off guard. "Uh, no. Do you?"

"No." Sean laughed. "And since there are only thirty minutes until the bell, I say we ditch."

"Sean Vega! You, the nephew of the only cop in Blackfin, suggesting we cut class?"

He leaned in. "If you really want to know, it's not my first time."

Then he gave her a cheeky grin and led her out through the side door. They both started running, across the lot and straight onto the sidewalk of Main Street.

"Maybe we should . . ."

But Sean was already one step ahead, turning so they were heading away from the weathered storefronts lining the street. They passed the candy store, whose door would only open when knocked upon with the rhythm of "Happy Birthday to You," and the secondhand bookstore, where every purchase came with a free spider in the bag. They ran on past Old Lady Brady sitting on her bench and up to the Point—the hill that cut off into an unnaturally sheer cliff face. The foot of the cliff was shrouded in a permanent fog, impossible to see either at night or during the day.

They were both red-faced and breathing hard by the time they reached the guardrail at the Point. It was roughly two hundred feet from the peak to the base, and the rail was a patchwork of old and new sections where a car must have driven through it, or the salt air had taken its toll.

This spot was also where a lot of kids came to make out, away from Main Street and prying eyes. Not that Sky was thinking about that, of course. Not at all.

Sky stood a few feet from the edge and stooped to pick up a pebble. She tossed it over the edge, watching it fall with a grace that made it look like it wasn't moving at all.

"I still can't get used to all the weird things that go on around here."

Sky looked up and found Sean wearing a bemused expression.

"You've only lived here a couple years. Give it another ten, and you'll be as freaky as the rest of us."

Sean smiled briefly. "Was I being paranoid, or was Miss Schwarz acting really weirdly back there?"

Sky nodded, glancing back down the hill. The road was deserted. "A little intense, yeah."

"I'm sorry if I made things worse for you. I know you hate it when people are talking about you."

Sky tugged her collar up. "I don't like it, but I'm also kind of used to it. It's been worse lately, though. Even among the freaks, the zombie girl is weird."

"You look a little tired, but I wouldn't go as far as calling you *zombie girl.*" Sean's hair blew into his eyes as he moved to stand next to her. "Did my sister keep you up all night gossiping or something?"

Sky fought her instinct to hide the steaming mess of weirdness her life had become. After all, Sean had dragged her cold, dead body out of the sea. He'd snuck into the woods with her late at night to track down an old gypsy lady, and he'd held on to her at the circus when she'd started to fade right in front of him. And in spite of it all, he was still here, still her friend.

In that moment Sky felt guilty for wanting more from Sean.

Sky picked up another stone and hurled it out to sea. It sailed in an arc before the water ended its journey.

"So, last night, I think I might have time traveled or something. . . ."

⚜︎

SEAN HAD ASKED all kinds of questions. Had Sky checked for footprints outside the house that might have shown she'd been sleepwalking? She hadn't, but neither had her father complained about cats messing up his vegetable garden that morning, so it was safe to assume she hadn't sleep-jumped from her balcony.

Had her father ever mentioned performing in a circus when he was younger? Certainly not. As far as Sky knew, her father had always been a mechanic—in France before he moved to the States after inheriting the Blood House from a distant relative.

Did she know how old her parents had been when they met? Sky didn't know that, either; her mother always talked as though she had never lived anywhere but Blackfin, so she'd assumed they had met when her father moved there. Had Sky recognized either of the voices she had heard whispering about murder above where she had materialized under the grandstand? No, although they *had* been whispering, and the band had been very loud, so she couldn't say for certain.

Did Sky have any idea who the ringmaster was? And why he had been staring at her? Other than the fact she had been wearing pajamas, Sky had no clue.

And finally: Was that where she had disappeared to for three months while everyone had thought Sky was dead? This, at least, she had an answer to. She was 100 percent certain she had *not* spent three months living in a circus. But she *had* been somewhere else, and the thought that she had no control over when or where she had disappeared terrified her. It must have been plain for Sean to see, as he'd pulled her closer to him.

Standing at the Point, talking to Sean with their fingers laced together, Sky felt something loosening inside her. It wasn't just that she trusted Sean not to treat her like the freak she'd always felt she was. Finally, now that her world had been completely turned around until she no longer knew for sure what was real and what wasn't, Sky didn't feel like she was on her own anymore.

The darkening sky finally forced them back into town, and Sky had to rush to make sure she was home when her parents arrived.

Sky said a reluctant good-bye to Sean at the fork where her road branched off from Provencher Street. As Sky turned into her driveway, she saw that her mother's car was already there.

Damn.

Sky breezed through the front door and into the kitchen as though nothing was out of the ordinary. "Hey, Mom, how was work?"

Lily looked up from where she had been staring into a glass of white wine, and Sky knew immediately that something was wrong. Her mother never drank anything other than coffee as a rule, which Sky had always blamed—at least partly—for her short temper.

"Oh, hey, honey. Sorry, I guess I spaced out for a minute there. I gave myself the afternoon off since the diner wasn't that busy." Sky thought for a moment that she'd managed to avoid any further questions that would lead to her having to flat-out lie about her after-school detour with Sean, but then Lily's eyes fixed on the gathering darkness outside the kitchen windows. "Where did you get to after school?"

"I felt a bit off during last period, and the school nurse wasn't there"—for all Sky knew, this was the truth—"so I took a walk to clear my head."

"Ah, okay. I hope you're feeling better now."

Now she knew something was really bothering her mother. Sky would never have gotten away with such a light grilling on a normal day, if normal days actually existed in Blackfin.

But what did and did not exist had become less tangible to Sky, like ribbons of light caught in a breeze, drifting through her fingers.

She caught one and tried to follow it.

"Mom, was somebody murdered here? Years ago, I mean?"

Sky's thoughts had wandered back to the overheard conversation under the bleachers, wondering whether the two she had heard conspiring had actually gone through with it. Because that would be a solid lead, something she could look into, research, try to figure out where—or *when*—she'd traveled to the previous night. And on her birthday.

Sky shuddered. As curious as she was to get to the truth of what had happened to her, the more she questioned it, and the more her grip on everything seemed to unravel.

"You mustn't listen to idle gossip, Skylar. What happened in this house was not your grandfather's fault," Lily said slowly.

The doorframe groaned faintly above her head, and Sky stepped quickly into the kitchen.

"I never met him, but your dad said he was a kind man, that he'd never do what he was accused of." Her mother winced as Sky slipped into the opposite seat, as though she hadn't meant to say anything at all.

This was not at all what Sky had expected. Could one of the people having a whispered conversation at the circus have been her grandfather? Was that the connection that had drawn her there?

Was the Blood House somehow responsible for Sky seeing the past? Shifting dimensions?

"This house was always called the Blood House, even before what happened. He *was* a butcher, after all."

Sky had known the house had historically always belonged to the Blackfin butcher. What now served as their garage had once been the butcher's shop, and the faint stink of raw meat still wafted up into Sky's room on a hot day. Thankfully hot days were rare.

She almost choked on her tongue. "You told me Dad inherited this house from a distant relative."

Lily looked up again at the reproach in her daughter's voice. "They *were* distant by the time they died. Gui hadn't seen his family in fifteen years." Lily's mouth hardened into a stern line as she looked accusingly at her wine glass. "Skylar, promise me you won't mention this to anyone else, especially your dad. I don't know who told you about it, but they're just raking over old bones. We all agreed a long time ago that we'd never talk about what happened." Lily frowned. "It would hurt your father a great deal to be reminded of what happened."

"You know I'd never do anything to upset Dad."

Lily gave a satisfied nod. "Good girl."

⁂

THE THOUGHT OF someone being murdered in her home made Sky shiver a little. She had always loved this house, loved the feeling that it held generations of memories before hers, memories from her own distant family. Or not-so-distant, according to her mother. But now it seemed those memories weren't quite what Sky had believed.

Sky was almost at her bedroom door when something brushed against her head, making her jump. The hatch to the attic hung open, the pull cord for the ladder swinging as though a hand had just released it.

"What are you trying to tell me now?" Sky wondered, not expecting a direct answer from the Blood House, and receiving none.

The ladder slid silently into place, and Sky hurried up it before her mother could come upstairs and catch her. Once through the hatchway, the smell of dust and old house greeted her. Sky pulled the ladder back up and closed the hatch, sealing herself in the musty darkness.

She turned, groping blindly for the cord to the bare bulb hanging overhead. She pulled the cord, and the bulb burned into life.

Boxes were strewn in rough piles under the eaves, some marked in Lily's neat script with words like *diner accounts* and *garage receipts*.

Sky mentally discarded those boxes, then stopped. If her mother wanted to hide something where Sky would never look for it, it would be just like her to mark the box *diner accounts*. Then again, the house and its secrets really belonged to Gui, and he would be more likely to mark it *Top Secret*.

"Start with the obvious, then."

She started with the boxes that looked the oldest—so dusty that she expected they would have dinosaur eggs inside. But most were filled with the dull things one might find boxed up in any attic—old sweaters, toys from when she was little, picture frames her mother had fallen out of love with over the years. She'd gone through as many musty-smelling sweater boxes as she could take and was about to move onto her mother's possibly deceptive *diner accounts* boxes when she pulled out the final sweater and found a wooden memento case hidden at the bottom. Its surface was scarred and pitted, bearing the initials GFR in one corner.

Guillaume François Rousseau.

The letters were crude, like they had been carved there by a child with a compass.

"Bingo?" Sky murmured uncertainly, setting the memento case on an old bureau under the single light. There was no complicated locking mechanism, just a hinge keeping the two halves of the case together.

Faded newspaper cuttings were packed inside the case, some with pictures under the headings. But they were all in French, and from the dates at the top of some of the articles, they were from way before Sky's encounter at the Big Top could have happened. Her heart sank a little—until one word caught her eye.

Kidnappé.

Who had been kidnapped? The image accompanying the article was of a family with three children—two girls with long, dark pigtails, and a little boy with bushy hair who looked about ten. The only remarkable thing about the family was the colossal size of the man.

"You must be Grandpa Rousseau," Sky realized. She stared at the man, so like her father in the way he stood with one big arm around his wife's shoulders, his eyes crinkled at the edges from years of smiling.

That's not the face of a murderer.

She unfolded the newspaper clipping and scanned the text.

Her French wasn't good enough to decipher most of it, but she at least confirmed her guess. The words *M. et Mme. Rousseau avec leurs enfants* were written in the second paragraph: *Mr. and Mrs. Rousseau with their children.*

It would have been hard to tell just from the grainy image, but now she could pick out her father's features in the little boy.

Sky flicked through the other articles. Some focused on the parents, but one image featured a man Sky had never seen before. He had a gaunt face with sunken eyes, and lips that looked ready to twist into a foul expression at any moment. *Recherché par la police* was written beneath the artist's sketch.

"Are you the kidnapper?" she asked the article, flipping it over to see whether there was anything else on the back.

That was when she saw it.

118

On the back of the article was another printed image, only this one looked like a promotional shot for *Le Cirque de Severin*, which had been copied to go with the news article. It featured a row of circus performers, all lined up in front of the Big Top with their ringmaster in the middle of the group. Even in the faded news copy, Severin's eyes bored into her.

Sky set the clippings aside, her head starting to ache from all the impossibilities. She flicked through the remaining contents of the memento case, picking out random photos of her dad with his two older sisters and their parents, watching him age and grow younger as the photos jumped back and forth through the years. Then she noticed something peculiar: her father never seemed to be more than ten years old in the pictures. And then what Lily had said downstairs in the kitchen made the pieces all fall into place.

"Gui hadn't seen his family in fifteen years."

The kidnapped child had been Sky's dad, and his family had never managed to find him. Had the ringmaster kidnapped her father, taking him along with the traveling circus? It made sense, except . . .

Except that the circus had come to Blackfin, where Gui's family were by then living in the Blood House.

The wooden boards of the attic floor moaned beneath her, a most melancholy sound.

"They must have moved here sometime after Dad was taken,"

Sky thought out loud, carefully putting all the cuttings and photos back into the memento case. "Until Dad inherited the house."

But then why would her father have inherited the house if he had a mother and two older sisters?

Unless they were the ones my grandfather murdered.

The Blood House had earned its name one way or another. And if the murder had been committed around the time the circus came to Blackfin, then it was somehow connected.

But what did that have to do with the fire in the woods, or Sky being chased off Blackfin Pier years later? The connection was there, she was certain. All she needed to do was see it.

❧ 12 ❧

WHATEVER OFFICER VEGA'S reason had been for letting those little creeps back out into the general population, Sky couldn't figure it out.

The Swivellers denied all knowledge of the grave disturbance, and couldn't be persuaded, threatened, or coerced into admitting they had removed the body that they found inside. That was, of course, assuming there had been a body inside it to begin with.

No use denying it. Someone who looked a lot like me got buried in that grave.

Her thoughts drifted back to the terrible dream she had of being trapped inside the coffin, and a cold finger of dread iced its way down her spine. *Had* that been a dream? Or had she in fact traveled to some other time, some other reality, and materialized inside the coffin with her other self's corpse?

Sky was so distracted she almost didn't notice she was nearing the Swivellers' house. Sky ducked her head to pass by on the way to Cam's, but she already knew it was too late. They'd spotted her, and were trickling like roaches out of their house to intercept her.

She picked up her pace until she was practically running. But the Swivellers kept up, separating so that two were on either side of her. Seeing no alternative, Sky stopped.

"What do you want?" Sky asked.

Randy Swiveller answered, his eyes moving like they had been oiled. "You got us into trouble."

"I did? How exactly do you work that out?"

Sky took an involuntary step away from him, only to find herself backed up against Colby Swiveller. His reptilian hands grasped her upper arms, and Sky tried to wrestle free. But for all that they appeared jointless, Colby, at least, was incredibly tenacious.

"Let me go."

"I say we fix what they say we done wrong, what do you think?"

Randy's gaze never wavered from her face as he spoke, his smile so broad Sky could see the gums of his back teeth.

"Put her back in the ground, you mean?" Colby's excited breath was disgustingly moist against her ear. Randy nodded.

"Let me go, you idiots!"

They ignored her, and Jordy and Felix each stepped forward and grabbed one of her legs. Sky screamed and kicked at them as her weight shifted, and she was hoisted between the four boys like an animal. They set off running up the hill, their knees battering her with every step.

"You can't do this!" Sky thrashed, really starting to panic. The Swivellers had always been creepy, but more or less harmless.

"Oh, we can, Skylar. You've already been officially dead, and ain't none but Jesus coming back from that gig."

They reached the cemetery within a minute, the old gate creaking open in welcome as the four boys carried her in.

Ohgodohgodohgodthey'rereallygoingtodoit.

Someone started giggling, and after a moment Sky realized it was her.

"Why's she laughing, Ran?"

Randy stared at her with his bug eyes and halted the others. "Dunno. Who can say what deaduns think?" He stared at her a moment, then pulled back his arm and slapped her hard across the face. Sky felt the sting of a split lip, and stopped laughing. "There, that fixed her. Right—in the hole."

The open grave had been covered by a large board and cordoned off with police tape, but Felix simply batted the tape out of the way and dragged the cover aside.

"Please—" Sky begged, but they weren't listening. The Swivellers threw her into the hole. She landed on her back, the wind knocked from her. All four boys stared down from one side of the grave, the mound of fresh earth that had been removed with the coffin on the other. The gray strip of sky was too bright, too vivid for winter in Blackfin.

"We should have brung a shovel," Jordy whispered. His words filtered down to Sky as though from far away.

"We can use our feet," Colby suggested, looking from one brother to another. Randy nodded, and the four disappeared from Sky's view for a moment. She scrambled to a half crouch, her back against the wall of the grave where the head of her coffin would have been.

Soil started to rain down in sharp bursts, making clouds of earth so that Sky had to hold the sleeve of her coat over her nose and mouth to breathe. Even then, her hot tears and blocked nose made her choke in a matter of seconds.

I need to get out of here.

Sky held her breath against the shower of grave soil. She jumped, trying to catch the lip of the hole, but her fingers slid off the dewy grass and she slid backward. Her wrist burned where she'd twisted it. Sky curled into herself, hugging her arms around her head until she could breathe a little without sucking in earth.

What the hell are they doing?

What had started as whoops of glee had turned into growls and snarls, like they were a pack of dogs and not four seriously twisted brothers. Stranger than that, though, was that the sound was almost familiar.

Soil continued to shower her for a few minutes, but the Swivellers were tiring from kicking at the mound. Sky could just about make out their labored breathing overhead, and wished they would choke on their own dust cloud.

She *also* wished they would get bored and go home so she could escape, but Randy's next statement sank any hope she had.

"I'll go home for the shovel."

Colby piped up eagerly. "Bring the whacker, too."

Sky wondered what exactly a *whacker* was, but the sound of Randy's feet running toward the cemetery gate told her she would find out soon enough. Her throat started to close.

But with Randy gone, the brothers' odd howling petered off, and Sky saw an opening. Although Randy wasn't the eldest Swiveller, his relative intelligence had made him the leader of their weird little gang. Without him there, Sky might be able to talk her way out of her own grave.

"Felix, I hurt my wrist. I need to go and put some ice on it, if you'd give me a hand to get out?" She tried to make her voice sound as cheerful as possible, like the whole situation had been nothing but a game. Looking up, she found his beady eyes staring back at her.

"Randy'd better hurry with the whacker," he said finally, and spat into the hole, missing Sky by a few inches. The brothers' faces disappeared again as they resumed kicking soil into the grave, and she was forced back into her fetal position in the corner. Her lungs burned as she tried to take shallow breaths, her panic fighting to make her gulp in the dust. But the throbbing in her wrist helped her to focus a little, and her chest stopped threatening to explode.

Yeah, because a sprained wrist is the worst of my worries right now. Why didn't I just stay home this morning?

Lightning crackled somewhere in the distance, and Sky became light-headed. She closed her eyes, but that only made it worse. The sound of the dirt landing on her faded, until she almost felt like she was somewhere else. Say, in her bed . . .

"Back away from the hole, boys!"

Sky jolted. She had never been so pleased to hear Officer Vega's voice.

Did I just start to fade out again?

Sky's heart pounded. She'd been about to drift back out of her life, either to that other existence where she'd lived an oblivious three months, or to the circus where strange men had chased her.

Yet even with the Swivellers' bizarre behavior, Sky clung to the moment. *I won't disappear. Not again.*

There was a moment of silence from the graveside, then Jordy, Colby, and Felix started whispering to each other. Sky didn't move.

"Back away, *now*. I caught Randy on his way back here with a shovel and a bat, and he's waiting in the back of my truck right now." *Ah. A whacker is a baseball bat,* Sky thought. "You're all going to come with me to Oakridge Station. Don't make me use this, boys."

That caught Sky's attention. Was Officer Vega holding a gun

on them? Should she let the police officer know she was down there so she didn't startle her into firing?

"Officer Vega," Sky yelled as best she could, her voice hoarse and choked with dirt. "I'm in the hole!" She lifted her hand to wave, and noticed that her sprained wrist didn't hurt at all anymore.

Weird.

"Is that Skylar?" There was no denying the horrified note in Officer Vega's voice.

"Sky?"

At the sound of Sean's voice, Sky heard his aunt curse under her breath. Sean's face appeared above her a moment later.

He leaned over the edge of the grave, his eyes widening as he spotted her crouched in the corner, caked in dirt.

"Oh my God, what did they do to you?" He turned his head to glare briefly at the remaining Swiveller brothers. One of them made a tentative kick at the mound again.

"Hey!" There was no arguing with Officer Vega's tone, and the soil cascade stopped. "I said back the hell up, right now!" This time, Sky could hear the shuffle of their feet as the Swivellers moved a few paces from the hole. "Sean, can you get her out of there?"

Sean reached down toward her. "Sky, grab my hands."

Sky stood, but didn't reach up to take them. "I don't want to pull you down here, too. Do you think maybe you could find a rope or a stepladder or—"

The next moment, Sean was in the hole with her, smears of dirt and grass stains covering his sweater. "Are you hurt anywhere?" He squinted at her.

"I'm fine, Sean. Honestly." *Tired, cold, and shaking like a leaf, but otherwise just dandy.*

"I'm going to kill—"

"Felix, right?" Officer Vega interrupted. "Didn't you get held back a year at school?" Felix grunted in response. "Good. That means you're eighteen."

There was a sound like a firecracker. Felix made a noise like a cat being strangled and thudded to the ground, even more boneless than usual.

"Now, do either of you two want to test how strict I am about not Tasering under-eighteens?" There was a pause, presumably while they shook their heads. "Good. Now get in the truck."

13

SKY WENT HOME with Sean in his Jeep after insisting she didn't need to go to the hospital in Oakridge. The last thing she wanted to do was spend hours waiting for doctors to come and prod and poke at her until they decided she was fine. Sky wasn't sure exactly *how* she was fine, but a hot shower that removed the ground-in dirt had revealed no bruises at all.

When Sky had point-blank refused to call either of her parents, she and Sean had reached a compromise: Sean would stay with Sky until her parents finished work, then Sky would tell them exactly what had happened.

"They'll find out as soon as Aunt Holly gets back from Oakridge anyway," Sean had pointed out, and Sky had to face the fact that he was right.

Sky dressed in sweatpants and an old sweater of her father's that reached right down to her knees and had to be worn with the sleeves rolled over several times. She had no energy to put into looking cute for the guy who had helped save her from being buried alive and was now sitting on her couch flipping through the music stations.

Sean looked up when he heard Sky coming downstairs. Now

that she'd turned herself from a mud monster back into a clean, human girl, Sean's dishevelment was more noticeable. He got up as she reached the bottom step, like he was her prom date waiting for her to make an entrance in a big froufrou dress.

"Hey, sorry, I should have asked if you want to go get cleaned up."

"That's okay. I cleaned up the worst of it in the laundry room." They both looked down at the green and brown smears covering the front of his sweater.

"I can get you one of Dad's shirts to wear?"

"One of yours would probably fit me better."

"I have a nice fluffy pink one that might suit you," Sky teased, and Sean shook his head, laughing.

He pulled his sweater off in a swift movement and tossed it to where his mud-caked Converse were sitting by the front door. The movement pulled the gray T-shirt Sean wore underneath up on one side, revealing a strip of skin above the waistband of his jeans before he smoothed it back down. Sky looked up before he could catch her staring at him.

"I'll be right back."

By the time she had returned with one of her father's smallest shirts, Sean was making tea in the kitchen. He put on the shirt and rolled the sleeves back like she had. Sean was tall enough that it didn't quite reach his knees, but he still looked ridiculous, and the way he fought a grin told Sky he knew it.

"Here," he said, handing her a mug of tea. They both blew the steam from their drinks before sipping in silence for a minute. "I'm happy to wait down here if you want to go and take a nap, you know. You don't need to keep me company."

You could keep me company while I take a nap, she thought, but banished the idea before it could turn into an all-out blush.

"How about we just go and watch TV instead?"

Sean nodded and followed her back into the family room, taking the seat next to her.

"Here, stretch out."

Sky's heart skittered around her chest as he maneuvered her to lie with her head on a cushion in his lap. "Comfortable?" Sky nodded up at him, and Sean flipped the blanket from the back of the couch down to cover her. "Good."

He put the TV on low, some kind of nature documentary that had crickets chirping faintly in the background. His hand ran down Sky's arm in a smoothing motion, over and over, lulling her until she drifted off to sleep.

❧❧❧

SKY'S PARENTS HAD naturally freaked when they found Sky asleep in Sean's lap, but they'd freaked out even more when they heard what the Swivellers had done. Sky listened from her bedroom as they talked to Officer Vega downstairs the next morning.

"As three of the four are juveniles and Skylar wasn't physically hurt," Officer Vega said, "I doubt they'll get more than a slap on the wrist, if I'm honest. But I have spoken with Principal Hemlock, and she agrees that having the Swiveller boys back at Blackfin High while Skylar is still a student would be out of the question."

"You're goddamn right it's out of the question!"

Officer Vega continued, "Principal Hemlock is arranging for them to be transferred to Oakridge High, with immediate effect. I have also recommended they be referred for psychological assessment."

"The Swivellers live less than a quarter of a mile from our house." Gui's deep voice sounded like he was barely keeping his temper in check. "Are you suggesting that our daughter be forced to relive that nightmare every time she—"

"Dad, please stop. I'm just fine, honestly." All eyes focused on Sky as she stepped into the family room, carrying her mother's smelling salts—just in case. "Well, I will be. The Swivellers are weird jerks, but there's nothing we can do about having to run into them from time to time." Gui raised an eyebrow, but Sky pressed on. "I'm not going to lie. I would be really happy to never have to look at any of them ever again. But this is a small town, and if we decided to run every weirdo out of Blackfin there'd be no one left." And with that, Sky grabbed her somehow freshly laundered red coat from the hook by the front door. "I'm going for a walk, and then I thought I'd come help out in the diner, if that's all right, Mom?"

The three adults looked at her like they weren't at all sure how to take her declaration. But Sky would not let the encounter with the Swivellers turn her into a quivering wreck. She'd survived worse, apparently.

Finally, her mother smiled.

"I'll see you there, my girl."

✦❦✦

SKY WIPED DOWN the coffeemaker for the seventeenth time and dumped the cloth next to it. She really needed a break from thinking about everything. Just for one day, she would like normalcy.

The bell rang to announce that another order was ready, and Sky went over to collect it.

"Table six," Deano lisped, and winked at her through the hatch from the kitchen. His eyes were a mismatch—one brown, one pale blue—and today he wore the blue on the right.

"Thanks, Deano."

Sky carried the food over to the table in the corner of the diner.

Jared sat alone in the booth, and smiled when he saw her.

"Oh, hey. I thought I saw you working back there. How are things?"

Sky set down the plate in front of him before answering. "Is this you *not* asking about the whole being-buried-alive thing that happened yesterday?"

He smiled and held up his hands. "You got me. Want to sit for a minute?"

Sky glanced back at the kitchen. The lunchtime rush was pretty much over, and they wouldn't miss her for a couple of minutes.

"I'll let you steal some of my fries?"

Sky slid into the booth opposite Jared and grabbed a french fry from his plate. "I guess I can join you for a little while."

Jared picked up his burger, looking at it from different angles like he wasn't quite sure how to attack it.

"Deano makes a mean burger," Sky said, watching as he took an enormous bite. She grabbed another fry and waited while he chewed.

"'Sgood." Jared swallowed his mouthful and took a drink. "So, you went to see the old gypsy woman."

Sky nodded, putting the pieces together. "Was that you out in the woods with the flashlight? Your VW?"

Jared tipped his head to one side while he chewed another mouthful.

"My van, yes. I saw tracks and figured I'd move my van in case I got reported for trespassing. But it wasn't me with a flashlight. Was someone else there with you?"

Sky heard the pointed note to the question, but wasn't sure what it meant. "I went with a friend."

He sucked his teeth as he wiped his mouth with a napkin. "And did you get the answers you wanted?"

She studied his face, the serious line of his mouth. The jewelry in his lip and nose matched his eyes, as though he was making a statement that he hid nothing. As much as there was something a little pushy about Jared, Sky could admit that she liked him. But that didn't mean she would share the things Madame Curio had told her.

"She didn't say an awful lot, no."

"Would you like me to come with you to speak to her again?"

Sky wiped her hands on her waitressing apron. "Why would you do that? And why would you being there help?"

Jared held up his hands. "I just thought it might be worth a shot, that's all. And I'm not working today. But whatever, that's cool."

Sky slid out from the booth and paused.

"Just give me two minutes to tell my mom I'm leaving, and I'll be right back."

Of course Sky wouldn't be telling her mother *where* she was going, or with whom.

She knew Sean had soccer practice on Sunday afternoons, so he wouldn't get her text until after dark, by which time Sky had every intention of being back. But as she called through the hatch to her mom, Sky hit SEND, so at least someone would know where she had gone—just in case.

Going back to see M Curio. I'm ok, Jared's with me.

Call u l8r.

❧ 14 ❧

THE FENCE GUARDING Blackfin Woods stared defiantly back at Sky as she inspected its perfectly straight, perfectly impenetrable, iron bars.

"What's up?" Jared, who had been quiet on the walk up the hill, leaned in to see what Sky was looking at.

"We bent the bars and went in through the fence last time, but someone's straightened them out again." She looked down at her heeled boots. "And no way am I climbing over in these."

Jared smirked. "I blocked the gap a few days ago. Don't want people sneaking into my woods whenever they feel like it."

Sky gave him an arch look. "*Your* woods? You've lived in Blackfin for five minutes."

"True. But I do live in there, and I don't like people sneaking up on me."

"Wait, you mean you actually *live* in there, in your van?"

"You make me sound as bad as the old gypsy," Jared said.

"You kind of are."

They carried on that way until Jared halted at the gates and fished a key from his pocket. He picked up the shiny padlock holding the chain in place and opened it with a *click*. The gates swung open without a sound, as though they had been recently oiled.

"How the hell do you have a key?" Sky stood still outside the gates.

He grinned. "Broke the old one off and replaced it with a new one."

Sky shook her head, even as she entered the gate and pushed it closed behind her. "Old Moley won't be happy." Jared clicked the padlock back into place.

"He hasn't noticed in the last three months, so I doubt he will anytime soon."

In daylight, there was nothing very terrible about the woods at all. Sky was beginning to enjoy the fresh, piney scent in the cold air, the snapping of twigs and rustle of fallen leaves, when they came to the clearing. The trees thinned to nothing around the church, where the earth was still too scarred by the fire to allow new growth.

A burning crackle greeted them as they rounded the corner of the church, and they found Madame Curio huddled next to a small fire, her tartan toga wrapped around her. From the mangled state of the tree in the ruin, it was obviously Madame Curio's primary source of firewood.

She looked up as Sky and Jared approached, but gave no other reaction to their presence.

"Madame Curio, do you remember me?"

The old woman rolled her eyes. "Yes, yes. What do you want now?"

"May we sit with you?" Jared practically shoved Sky toward her. Sky glared at Jared, and sat on the log facing Madame Curio. "You saw what happened to my friend here the night she was meant to have died—"

"Not *meant to*. Did. But not this one, the other."

Jared sighed. "Yes. That night. Can you explain exactly what happened?"

Madame Curio narrowed her eyes at Jared. "I suppose I could. For a smoke."

"Sorry, I don't smoke."

Her mouth puckered like a cat's rear end. "You did not come with the best bargaining hand, did you?"

Jared reached into the pocket of his jacket. "I have ten bucks that says otherwise."

The old woman's eyes lit up. "Give!"

"After you've told Skylar everything she wants to know."

Madame Curio pouted, sat back, and slammed her arms folded across her chest. "Told her. They chased her and she jumped off."

"Wait, *who*—"

"Four of 'em. Growling."

"You're sure about this?" Something about Jared's angry tone made both Sky and Madame Curio jump.

"He's very rude, isn't he?" Madame Curio leaned forward and

whispered dramatically. "You are the product of both your parents, Skylar. Your gift is like Severin's, and not."

Sky watched the old woman's eyes glaze over, as though someone had drawn a curtain over her mind and she was now closed for business.

"Is that it?" Jared appeared more put out by the abrupt end to the conversation than Sky was, and his interest in helping her was starting to feel a little too involved.

"Come on, we'd better go. It will be getting dark soon." Sky stood, swiping the loose bark fragments from her coat.

Jared stood, too, and turned to Madame Curio. He had just pressed the ten-dollar bill into her hand when she shrieked and leaped to her feet.

"You're his! HISSSSS!"

With a dexterity uncommon in thousand-year-old women, Madame Curio climbed the rubble behind her and stood in the empty shell of the window casing, pointing at Jared with a shaking finger.

"You belong to *Gage*!"

Jared blanched.

"Wait, Jared—what does she mean?"

Jared didn't answer Sky's question. With a glare at Madame Curio, he strode back the way he and Sky had come.

Sky didn't know what to do.

"And you can bugger off, too!"

The decision taken out of her hands, Sky gathered her coat around her and went running after Jared. She followed his tracks back to the gates and saw him waiting on the other side. Sky's cell started ringing the moment she stepped past the fence. Using her teeth to remove her glove, she answered it.

"*Hurro?*"

"What's wrong? Where are you?"

Sky took the glove from her mouth with her free hand and signaled to Jared that she'd be a minute.

"Nothing's wrong. I'm just on my way home. Are you okay?"

There was silence on the other end of the line while Sean took several deep breaths. "I was worried something had happened to you."

Sky turned to face away from where Jared was waiting. "I was going to call as soon as I got home to let you know I'm okay."

Again, there was a long silence. "Who is Jared, anyway?"

"He works with my dad at the garage—"

"I know that, Sky. I mean, who is he *to you*?"

Sky's heart banged against her rib cage. Was that jealousy in Sean's voice? It was hard to tell over the phone. "Just a friend, Sean. Hardly even that, really. I've only met him a couple of times."

"After everything that happened yesterday, you didn't think it might not be the best idea to go sneaking into the woods with some-one you *barely know*?" Sky had never heard Sean sound really angry before, but she gathered this was what it sounded like. "This town is full of *freaks*, Sky! You can't trust any of them—"

"Freaks like me, you mean?" Sky's pointed question cut Sean dead in the middle of his rant.

"I didn't say that. I just can't believe you'd be so damn irresponsible, going off with some strange guy into the woods! What if something had happened to you? How could you be so—"

"I'm going to hang up now, Sean. I'll see you in school, I guess."

Sky's eyes became hot with tears. She rubbed at them jerkily, not letting them fall. Of course Sean would dump her in with the rest of the weirdos in Blackfin. The town was a part of her makeup, would always be, but it wasn't that way for Sean.

She switched off her cell and shoved it into her coat pocket before hurrying to catch up to Jared.

"Let's go."

"Are you all right?" he asked.

"Just dandy," she huffed. "But what did Madame Curio mean back there? Who is Gage?"

Jared didn't look at Sky. "I have no idea."

They walked the rest of the way in silence.

❧❧❧

SKY DIDN'T SWITCH her phone back on until the next morning. She had three missed calls from Sean, followed by a text when he'd given up calling.

I'm sorry.

What did that mean? Sorry for upsetting her? Sorry that she was a freak and he could never *really* like someone like her? Sorry for caring enough to get angry that she hadn't waited for him to go with her to the woods?

After tossing and turning the previous night while she went over everything in her head, Sky realized that was the only explanation for why he'd gotten angry. She had known since the night of her party that he must have *some* feelings for her, otherwise he'd never have fought Randy. But the fact remained that when it came down to it, what really hurt was that Sean was right. She was as *Blackfin* as they came.

And then there were all the weird things Madame Curio had said. Who was *Gage*, and what did Jared have to do with him?

Sky had English first period, so was spared the awkwardness of seeing Sean right away. Except that Bo was heading for the seat next to her.

Sky let her head fall forward onto the desk.

"Hey, I'm not even going to ask what's got you all in a funk with loverboy, so don't give me the drama-flails."

Sky rolled her head to one side, looking up at Bo suspiciously. "You're not?"

"No." Bo rustled around in her bag and thrust a wad of papers across the desk. "I copied my notes for you from physics last week, seeing as you skipped out. It was all the stuff we need for the mid-term on light refraction."

"Huh?"

Bo jabbed at the papers with a blue fingernail. "Remember when Miss Schwarz did that thing with the glass of water and a pencil to show how light bends . . ." Her voice trailed off. "Oh, right. You weren't actually here for that."

But Sky *did* remember it. "The one where it looked like the pencil bent at a funny angle where it entered the water?" Wherever Sky had been, she had seen the same demonstration. It figured that that would be the one thing that stayed the same, no matter which version of her life she was living.

"That's the one. Apparently we need to know that shit for the midterm."

It had not exactly been the highlight of Sky's academic year so far, but the theory had stuck with her. They had used crystals and other transparent objects to test how their dimensions affected how the light bent, or even split into its component hues.

Like whatever angle the light decides to hit the prism affects what the light will become, splitting it and sending it off on different paths.

"Decisions, decisions," Sky said to herself, staring at Bo's hastily scrawled diagram in front of her.

Decisions like whether she should actually try to time travel or whatever it was she was doing, so she could find out more about what happened in the Blood House, and who had tried to kill her. Or whether she should push Jared to tell her who this Gage guy was that he supposedly *belonged* to. And what to do about Sean.

"It's not always a decision," Bo said next to her, bringing Sky out of her thoughts. "Sometimes things just happen that we can't do anything about. I know that. But if it *is* your choice, please remember that people care about you, Sky, and we'll help you if you let us. If you stick around so we *can* help you." Bo cleared her throat, looked down at the desk in front of her. "Jeez, stop staring at me like we're having a moment or whatever."

Sky started to reassure her that she wasn't going anywhere—at least, not if she could help it—but Ms. Wooky stopped right in front of their desks before Sky could say more than a word.

Sky's doubts still lingered when the last bell rang. She found Sean already waiting for her by the school gates. He leaned against the gatepost, the collar of his parka pulled high against the wind. He pointed up toward the roof of the school once Sky had reached him. The weathervane had turned its back on their conversation, pointedly staring out to sea despite the strong breeze that should have steered him to look over the parking lot.

"Looks like Silas is mad at me, too."

Sky hunched her shoulders and watched the toe of her boot scrunch the gravel of the path next to the school gate. "I'm not mad at you, Sean." *Not* just *mad at you, anyway. I'm also mad at Jared, the crazy old gypsy in the woods, and life in general.* "And Silas is just a chunk of metal."

He laughed. "You *are* mad at me. But please be mad because I used a poor choice of words and was a jealous idiot, not because I think you're a freak—because I just don't. And I don't think you're irresponsible. Of course you've got other guy friends, why wouldn't you have? I just freaked out after hearing Cam go on and on about how *amazingly awesomely hot* this Jared guy is and kinda sorta lost my temper a little bit." Sky couldn't help laughing as he shuffled his feet on the gravel.

"I'm sorry for being an idiot," Sean said. "Come with me to Winterfest in Oakridge this weekend?"

Sky searched Sean's face. "Are you asking me on a date?"

He nodded. "I've always been asking you on a date. Every time." Sean swallowed loudly. "If you'd like to . . . I mean, if you'd rather it wasn't a date, we could make it more of a group thing—"

"I want to. Go on a date, I mean. With you."

Sean let out a long breath. "Good."

❧ 15 ❧

FOR THE NEXT four days, Sky managed not to run into the psychopathic brothers who had tried to bury her alive. Nor did she accidentally dematerialize and end up in an alternate version of her life. She also managed to stay within her own time period, avoiding circus ringmasters and whispering murderers, and was altogether . . . normal. Even Sky's mother seemed to have relaxed a little, and hadn't done more than blink when Sky told her parents she was going to Winterfest with Sean. On a date.

She *may* have implied that the outing was more of a group event. But Sean's name was specifically mentioned, so Sky reassured herself that she hadn't *technically* told a lie.

Instead, Sky had gone to school, hung out with Cam and Bo, and helped out at the diner when the Thursday Special drew in a larger crowd than usual.

Sky was happy. Happier than she'd been since before her disastrous birthday party.

But happiness held its own terror, because it meant that if she woke up one morning suddenly *back* in the life she'd lived for three months while a corpse that looked a lot like her rotted in Blackfin Cemetery, she'd be miserable again. And she still wouldn't have the answers she wanted.

But perhaps if she put it all behind her, stopped digging for things beyond her reach, she would get to keep her happiness.

"You look nervous, *coco.*"

Sky looked up from staring at the contents of her closet to see her dad filling the doorway. "Nervous?" She laughed nervously, completely undermining the nonchalance she'd been aiming for.

Her dad walked in and held out a pair of what looked suspiciously like jeans.

"I recovered these from your mother's last spree."

Sky's mouth dropped open. Gui had sneakily rescued some of her clothes from her mother's fashion tyranny?

"You cannot ice-skate in a skirt. What if you were to fall and skin your knees? It's simply a matter of safety."

He shuffled his feet, clearly not comfortable about being so underhanded, even if it was for his daughter's sake. Sky took the jeans from him and hugged them to her chest.

"I'll make sure she never knows."

Gui grinned sheepishly before kissing her on the forehead. "We do what we must for a quiet life, *n'est-ce pas?*" He turned as though to leave, but hesitated. "I will be having a fatherly talk to this young man you are sneaking out with, just as soon as the opportunity presents itself. Only to make sure he is familiar with the rules of living a quiet life, you understand."

"Dad!"

He shook his head and grinned. "I promise not to frighten him too badly, *coco*."

"I'm more worried about what Mom will say, to be honest."

Gui sighed. "Her objections aren't for the reasons you think. She only worries for your happiness. Her own childhood was not a happy one, and she wants you to be safer and happier than she ever was. You are our little girl, and always will be. *C'est tout*."

Sky wasn't sure she agreed with Gui's assessment, but she was spared having to comment by her mother's voice bellowing from downstairs.

"Gui! You've walked motor oil through the house *again*! Is it so goddamn difficult to take your goddamn boots off . . ."

This did not bode well for Gui, though he waggled his eyebrows in mischief. "Not always a quiet life, eh? *Le petit tyran* is out for blood, so I suggest you change quickly and use an *alternative* route to go and meet up with your young man." He nodded toward the french windows. Sky smiled as she listened to his retreating footsteps, then did exactly as he'd suggested.

THE ROAD TO the neighboring town wound up through the mountains encircling Blackfin, like it was a secret to be kept hidden from the rest of the world. Frequent and lethal drops punctuated the snaking ascent into the Lychgate Mountains.

Sky watched the town falling away behind them as Sean drove. He went slowly, avoiding the ice patches that had sent plenty of drivers plummeting from the high roads. They passed the post marking the town limits—the post where the WELCOME TO BLACKFIN sign should have been, except that the locals took it down every time the town council replaced it. There was no need to *encourage* people to visit, after all.

Sean pulled in at the side of the road as they reached the highest point, giving Sky a *follow me* look as he slid out of the car, his hair instantly whipping into a curly tangle as the wind hit him.

Sky joined him as he leaned against the back of the Jeep, looking out over the twisted townscape of Blackfin. The houses looked like precariously stacked playing cards, balancing against the hillside while they waited for a gust of wind to carry them off into the sea. From this height, Sky saw the thirteen black dots of the cemetery cats lazing on top of the tombstones lower down the mountain slope. Further still, the school teetered at the seafront, with Silas's iron form spinning crazily on the roof.

Sky drew her coat closer, then felt the added warmth of Sean's arm wrapped around her waist.

"I like the view from up here," he said, his voice low next to her ear.

"It's kind of pathetic to think how many times I've left Blackfin. Maybe ten times in my whole life, and even then it was only to go as far as Oakridge or Camberly. It's like there's this whole world I hear about and read about in books, but for all I know, maybe there isn't really anything outside this weird, tiny dot of land."

Sean squeezed her to him. "There is definitely more to see than Blackfin, but it does have its own unique appeal."

Sky angled her head so she could look at him. "You've never told me much about St. Louis. What was it like growing up there?"

He gave her a sideways glance. "Different from here. Not as many ghosts or crazy people. Not *Blackfin* crazy, anyway."

"Do you miss it?"

"Sometimes," he said. "I keep in touch with my friends online—when the frigging internet works in this town—and it's not like I can never go back there." He fell silent, but Sky sensed there was more coming. "I miss my parents, though. Or at least . . . I don't know, being part of a family."

"Don't you feel that way, living with Cam and your aunt?"

"Of course. I love them both to bits. But it seems like I'm just passing time or something. My parents are doing incredible re-search on their expedition in the Himalayas, and I'm so proud of them for that. But I can't help resenting them sometimes. Cam's her own whirlwind, and I've never met a woman more independent than Aunt Holly, and I just feel . . . unnecessary, I guess."

"I don't think you're unnecessary, Sean."

He looked at her, and that spark of mischief was back in his eyes. "No?"

Sean spun her so that his arms bracketed her against the car. Then neither of them were laughing.

"Promise me you won't disappear this time, okay?"

Sean kissed Sky without waiting for her answer. His lips were warm, and tasted of lazy smiles and strawberry laces. His thumbs smoothed down her cheeks and throat like he had to make sure she was real, was still there with him.

I've never been kissed like this before, Sky thought, tingles traveling from her head to her toes. *I can't believe I'm actually kissing Sean Vega.*

It was the first kiss they should have had, without the ugliness of the fight with Randy and the blood-tang of split lips, without the chemical taste of the spiked punch bowl between them.

This was exactly what Sky wanted.

She moved her hands from where they hovered at her sides and ran them up Sean's back. She felt his muscles flex in response, so she did it again.

He broke the kiss, his breathing terse, and grinned at her.

"I've wanted to kiss you for two years," Sean whispered, his lips barely brushing against hers. "I thought I'd never get the chance."

Sky gazed into his eyes, saw them looking for her reaction.

Then she kissed him, putting everything she couldn't say out loud into it as their bodies pressed together. A gust of wind whipped her hair against both their necks until Sean caught the strands and threaded his fingers through them.

His smile only accented his kiss-reddened mouth when he leaned back and took a strawberry lace from his pocket and snapped it in two, giving her half.

"This will be the first time I try ice-skating," he admitted.

Sky jumped into the passenger side of his Jeep and grinned at him. "I'll make sure you don't fall flat on your face."

⚜

THE FIRST SATURDAY of Winterfest always drew a crowd in Oakridge. They had to wait in line for almost half an hour before reaching the kiosk attendant, who favored them with a scowl upon seeing their Blackfin High student IDs.

"Is there some kind of problem?" Sean said, smiling.

The attendant shook his head and handed them their skates without a word. Trying not to think about the line of people still staring at their backs, Sky felt Sean's fingers link with her own as they made their way down to the rink.

"People are always like that when they realize you're from Blackfin," Sky whispered, feeling the need to explain the attendant's rudeness, but Sean just laughed.

"Oh, I know. I'm not *that* new to town."

Sean stopped Sky as she was about to head out onto the ice.

"You go ahead, I just want to take a picture of you out there before I stumble out like an ape and embarrass us both."

"All right. But I'm coming to get you if you're not out there in two minutes, Sean Vega. Besides, it's easier if you have someone to pull down onto the ice with you." Sky laughed and drifted into the circling skaters, her coat flapping behind her as she picked up speed.

Sky had never been afraid of falling. She'd taken her share of tumbles as she was learning how to skate, but the bruises faded quickly and the feeling of traveling so fast across the ice, making loops and turns as she found her rhythm, was more exhilarating than anything else she'd ever done. That was, up until she had kissed Sean Vega at the highest peak of the Lychgate Mountains.

She lost sight of Sean after making a couple of laps and had to scan the faces of the people outside the frozen arena, searching for him in the crowd. Sky soon spotted him—or at least part of him, as he held the cell phone out in front of his face while he took her photo. Sky twirled, laughing as she caught sight of the flash across the ice, and made her way back to where she'd started. But as she approached the hop-out point, she realized something had changed.

Sean was no longer standing where he'd been moments ago. Sky almost stopped dead, but was bussed along by a group of kids who narrowly avoided plowing into her. She moved slowly around the edge, almost tripping when she noticed some of the faces fading in and out, as though a light were being shone on them one second and gone the next. Sky pushed herself away, faster. The faces blurred, then went spinning as she clipped the skate of another girl.

Lightning writhed around her, and was gone in a blink, like something had cracked open.

Standing where Sean had been, Sky saw Cam and Bo huddled together. Only they weren't at the edge of the ice rink, and Sky couldn't feel the frozen slide beneath her feet anymore.

Bo's hand was on Cam's shoulder. At first it looked as though she was just comforting Cam, but then Sky noticed her white knuckles, like it was actually Bo who clung to Cam for support. They stood at the front of a crowd of people, all dressed in black as though they were going to a funeral.

A funeral?

Another moment, another flash, and Sky was plunged into darkness. She reached out with her hands, feeling nothing through her woolen gloves, but the cloying warmth against her face and neck told her she wasn't outside. A light blazed to life ahead of her, spotlighting a figure dressed all in black. She blinked against the brightness, breath catching in her chest as the figure turned to face her. It was the man she had seen at the circus, his face a deathly shade of white, eyes piercing her from the shadow of his bowler hat. He grinned, sending a splinter of ice traveling down Sky's spine.

He wants something from me. Something bad.

The thought burned in her head, seemingly from nowhere, but she would have bet anything she was right. The light blinked off, and Sky experienced a moment of blinding darkness before she was back on the ice, stumbling as her momentum pulled her forward and she narrowly avoided barreling into another skater.

I need to get off the ice, she thought, looking for the hop-out again. A flicker just above her head, and now she saw Cam and Bo and her parents, the faces of all the people she'd known her entire life in Blackfin flashing in and out like sparks, too quick for her eyes to follow.

Sky squinted against another flash, and another, like lightning, or a really powerful camera.

"Sky."

She lost sight of them again, the flashes of cameras and kids with glow sticks and the fluorescent lights overhead blending together in an overwhelming, pulsing web of light.

"Skylar!"

Something crashed into her. Sky's landing was much warmer and softer than she'd expected, and she looked down to find Sean lying winded under her.

"It took . . . forever . . . to reach you. Thought you'd . . . vanish before I . . ."

Then she understood. It hadn't worked.

Sky wanted to scream.

The weirdness had sought her out, tracked her down, and dragged her back into its embrace, even here, outside the limits of Blackfin. She'd been on the verge of disappearing again, vanishing into whatever strange universe she'd glimpsed in the swirling pattern of faces.

What did I just see? Was that where I've been for the last three months, some other version of now? And what does that man with the white face want with me?

Sky's heart pounded in her chest.

The skaters around them looked down worriedly to see if they were okay, but continued their leisurely circles as Sean started laughing underneath her.

"Is it all right if I say I hate ice-skating?"

Sky couldn't laugh along with him. She helped Sean get to his feet, trying her best to keep him from stumbling as they made their way back to the rink side.

"I saw . . ." Sky stopped. She had no idea how to explain what she'd seen. All the unanswered questions kept piling up on top of her, burying her, until Sky had no choice but to try and dig her way out.

"You saw what?"

Just a couple of weeks ago, Sky would have been able to put her hand on her heart and swear she'd never seen Sean look anxious for one moment of the time he'd lived in Blackfin. Now she was starting to recognize the fine lines that framed his mouth when he was worried, and she hated that she was the cause of them.

"I'm so sorry, Sean."

He frowned. "Sorry for what?"

For complicating your life. For being a massive freak.

Sky shook her head, forcing a smile. "Never mind. Let's go get rid of our skates and see if they have any hot chocolate over at the food stall. Hot chocolate fixes everything, you know."

※✿❀❁✿※

SKY LAY IN bed, wanting to kick something.

Maybe if she could travel back to the circus again, she would be able to find out how what had happened there was connected to what was happening to her here, now. Why she was drifting in and out of her life like a kite caught by the wind.

She pictured the Big Top, the smells and sounds of circus life surrounding her. Then her parents, how young they'd looked standing outside the great tent. Her father's soft words, *in your condition*, played over in her mind.

Sky's mother had been pregnant.

It hadn't been noticeable, so Lily couldn't have been far along in the pregnancy, and the chilly air outside the Big Top meant it must have been January or February—only sixteen years ago.

Which meant someone had been murdered in the Blood House within her lifetime, too. But was it a coincidence? It seemed unlikely, but she couldn't fathom how she played a part in events that had happened before she'd actually been born.

Okay. So whenever I've . . . traveled, it's been to some point in my life. Either in the past, or another version of now.

But why?

Sky stared at the ceiling, debating. It hadn't taken any deliberate effort on her part to travel there the first time, so surely if she focused on letting herself fade. . . .

Should I try to go back to the circus? Is it worth it just to get a few answers?

If letting it go, not questioning what happened on the night of my birthday, puts it all to rest and lets me get on with my life, isn't it worth it?

But maybe if I just go back there once, it will all somehow make sense.

The pulsing light that forked across her ceiling seemed to think so. It tangled and formed a web in front of her. Sky felt herself fading just as the light snaked down the wall and touched her with an icy finger, and the world split open around her.

❧ 16 ❧

SKY EXPECTED TO see the underside of the grandstand seating again. Maybe even a trickle of orange soda dropping toward her eyeball. Instead, she found Jared peering down at her.

Dressed in a warm coat, boots, and jeans, he took a step back to give her room to get up. They were in Blackfin Woods. The lights and music of the circus drifted faintly from the clearing a few hundred meters away, but otherwise, the woods were silent.

"Do you know where we are?"

Jared's tone was curious, as though his being suddenly alone with Sky in the middle of the woods with a supposedly derelict circus very much in full swing in the near distance was nothing more than an intriguing turn of events.

Sky wiggled her toes in the grass where dew had gathered. There was not a lick of frost anywhere. In fact, Sky found that even in only her camisole and pajama bottoms, she wasn't really cold.

"This isn't the same time as it was before," she said, more to herself than to answer Jared's question. "Everything's different."

A little ways from where they stood, Sky spotted the church spire rising straight and strong through the trees. There, at its peak,

Silas sat watching. Except Sky could somehow tell the weathervane wasn't haunted in this time, in its original spot on the church.

Weird.

Still, she waved hello—just in case.

"What do you mean? Where are we?"

Sky looked at Jared and pointed to the circus. "We've gone back in time. Something about that circus, or the people *in* the circus, is connected with how someone tried to kill me. I don't know how it ties together, or even why you're here this time, but as you *are*, you might as well help me get some answers."

"Sure. Come on, let's check it out."

They made their way carefully through the woods to the forest of pitched tents.

Although the music was playing and the circus lights flashed garishly above their heads, Sky had the impression that the main events weren't happening at the moment, and the crowds were yet to come. Instead of heading straight for the Big Top, Jared gestured for them to walk through the line of stalls making up the midway. The smell of popcorn and cotton candy and other sticky sweet things filled her nostrils, and she stared at the glass-fronted display of the doughnut vendor's stall.

"Only two bucks per half dozen, sweetheart," the boy manning the stall said in heavily accented English, though Sky couldn't identify the accent. "Or free if you give me a kiss." The boy grinned, revealing a set of teeth that had been filed into sharp points. Sky hurried on after Jared.

"Look!" Sky pointed farther along the row to where a kiosk draped in heavy fabrics bore the sign MADAME CURIO: TAROT, PALMISTRY, AND DIVINATION. $5 PER SESSION.

"I don't suppose you happen to have five bucks, do you?"

Jared patted himself down, checking the pockets of his coat, but came up empty.

"Nada."

"Damn. She might be less crazy now."

A small boy raced past them, his little legs thundering along as he squealed in delight. A woman who had to be his mother followed a moment later, red hair flaring out behind her as she called out, "Jimmy!" in a voice that was oddly familiar. They had both disappeared before Sky could put her finger on it.

"Why don't you just go and talk to her anyway?" Jared asked. Sky looked at him dubiously. "What's she going to do, run away screeching? If we really have gone back in time, your death-that-wasn't hasn't even happened yet."

Sky could see his point. She crossed the thoroughfare to the kiosk and poked her head inside. Madame Curio sat in the stuffy interior, eating what appeared to be a blue Popsicle. Despite the fact that this was sixteen years earlier than when Sky had last seen Madame Curio, the old woman looked just as old and weathered.

At least she's wearing clothes now, Sky thought. The old gypsy's eyes were heavily lined with kohl, her pale irises making her look like some kind of bird as she peered up at Sky.

"Welcome, child. Five dollars for your future."

Sky fiddled with the lace edge of her camisole. "Uh, I don't actually have five dollars."

Madame Curio's eyes narrowed. "What *do* you have?"

Besides her pajamas, the only thing Sky was wearing was a woven leather bracelet Cam had given her for her birthday. Madame Curio unsnapped the fastening and whipped the bracelet away, secreting it in the folds of her skirt.

"That will do. Sit."

Sky perched on what felt like an overturned crate, the hard seat only thinly covered with a piece of frayed velvet. Jared stayed at the opening to the kiosk, stooping to watch what was happening inside. Madame Curio didn't even acknowledge him. She held out her hand to Sky and nodded for her to do the same. Sky put her hand in the palm of the old woman's and waited. For a long moment, Madame Curio didn't move or speak. She didn't even appear to be breathing, and somehow all the sounds of music and voices and the general hubbub of the circus faded to nothing.

Am I fading out again? Sky wondered, but didn't have that insubstantial feeling that usually accompanied her fade-outs.

"Your parents have lied to you, many times." Madame Curio spat to one side after announcing this, narrowly missing a cat, which Sky hadn't noticed curled up in the corner. "But their lies no longer serve to protect you. I see a time, years from now, when you are sixteen"—Madame Curio looked up at Sky, apparently baffled by the contradiction—"when you will save your father's life, but this will bring you danger. Other hand."

Madame Curio gestured impatiently until Sky laid her left hand with its palm facing upward over the old woman's.

"A boy will be both a tether and a joy in your life." She looked up and held Sky's eye. "There are those who would try to keep you apart."

Sky said nothing.

"There is no way for him to save you, but he will try."

"Ask her who you need saving from," Jared whispered next to her. Madame Curio said nothing, so Sky cleared her throat and asked the question. But the old woman had reached behind her, and now held a crystal ball in front of her face. For a moment, Sky saw the distorted image of Madame Curio's face through it. But the light seemed to shift and hit it at a different angle, and the face in the ball seemed to twist and change, until it became a murky orange skull, its empty eye sockets and lipless grin mocking her. The old woman dropped it.

"Get out."

"But I just need to know who—"

"OUT."

Sky scrambled from the kiosk, trailed by Jared. Madame Curio pointed a shaking finger at her.

"You had a worm in your head, girl. A WORM."

With that, Madame Curio ducked back inside the kiosk and pulled the flap down, closing herself in. A moment later a pale, weathered hand snaked out from behind the flap and flipped the sign so that it read: MADAME CURIO: CLOSED FOR SPIRITUAL REFLECTION.

"Guess that was a dud," Sky said, turning to look for Jared, only to find that he had vanished. She made a full circle, feeling like a twirling fool in her lace-edged pajamas, but there was no sign of him.

"*Jared?*" she hissed, trying not to draw attention to herself but doing so all the same. Sky smiled sheepishly at the small boy who was staring up at her. He appeared to have given his mother the slip for the moment.

"Who are you?" He pinned her with his gaze in the way no normal three-year-old should have. "You don't fit."

Sky sighed, giving up on finding Jared for the moment. "Tell me about it. Do you know where the ringmaster is right now?"

The boy turned his head and drew in a breath in preparation for yelling.

"Wait, wait! Don't shout for him! Can you just tell me where he is?"

The boy thought it over, dark eyes studying her. Then he grinned.

"I'll tell you where he is," he said. Then he pointed over Sky's shoulder.

"Well, hello, *chère.*" The smell of smoke mingled with the cotton candy sweetness around them. Severin leaned against a tent pole, a slim black cheroot dangling from between his lips. Otherwise, he was dressed identically to when Sky had first seen him in the Big Top, minus the tall top hat. The glint in his eyes was exactly the same, however: a mix of curiosity, deviousness, and amusement. "I was wonderin' when you'd show up again."

Severin ushered Sky away from the midway. He opened the door to an old-fashioned trailer and beckoned her to follow. Sky didn't move.

His head reappeared at the doorway a moment later, looking thoroughly confused. "What is the matter?"

"I'm not going into a trailer with a strange man," Sky answered, holding her ground despite the hammering of her heart. This man might not *look* threatening, with his blue eyes and dimpled grin, but something about him rang seven kinds of alarm bells with Sky. It wasn't that he gave off a *predator* vibe—not at all. It was his voice. There was something so familiar about it, even though his accent, which held the deep, lazy rhythm of the Mississippi, wasn't anything she'd come across before in Blackfin.

Sky was *almost* certain his voice had been one of those she'd overheard whispering of murder the first time she had materialized at the circus, but there was no way she could learn more without actually talking to him.

"I am Augustus William Severin the Third, ringmaster of this here circus." He grinned and bowed from the waist. "And you are?"

Sky narrowed her eyes. "Skylar."

"And now we are no longer strangers, *chère*. Come, it'll be a sight easier for us to converse without having to shout through the door, don't you think?" Severin sighed theatrically and retreated inside his trailer where Sky could no longer see him. "Come in whenever you get tired of hanging around out there."

Sky stood outside the trailer in her bare feet and nightclothes, feeling like a genuine idiot, for all of five seconds before she hurried inside. She found Severin at a bench table, two cups of green tea in front of him and another black cheroot in his hand.

He held up a silver case and offered one to Sky, smiling wryly when she didn't move.

The old wooden trailer had a narrow bunk at the back and the table where he now sat, and every other spare inch had been packed with strange items. Sky counted at least seven clocks of various sorts and sizes, leather-bound books with titles like *The Alchemist's Guide to Electrical Conduction* and *Legacy of the Druids* along with what appeared to be legal volumes piled high up the walls until they wobbled with the shifting of her feet on the floorboards. Old-fashioned packing cases were stacked in one corner with an empty birdcage on top, although on second glance Sky realized it wasn't empty—a paper crane had been perched on the swing, its beak pointing straight at her.

"Aw, *chère*. You'll catch a face full of wrinkles if you keep pulling it like that. You've nothin' to fear from me."

It was difficult not to just watch Severin, the way he held his cheroot so the smoke curled upward in spirals, his eyes sharp and focused even when half-lidded.

"Much as I enjoy the scrutiny," he drawled, flicking ash into a glass vase on the table, "I'm sure you didn't come back here just to watch me smoke."

Sky cleared her throat and edged toward the table. Severin followed the movement with his eyes, but was otherwise completely still, as though he was used to being around animals that spooked easily.

"Are you going to kill me?"

Severin laughed, and it was as musical-sounding as the circus bells. "Now why in the world would I do that?"

Sky laced her fingers together in her lap, her knuckles white. "I don't know you. I don't know what you want."

"Firstly, *chère*, you came here looking for me, so it seems that you're the one who's wanting something. Secondly, if it sets your mind at ease, I've never killed a soul in my life. I can think of better ways to pass a good time."

She studied him a moment longer. Nothing about him was threatening in the slightest, but that in itself felt strange. "Why were you staring at me the other night, in the Big Top?"

His mouth twitched in a suppressed smile. *"The other night* was nigh on three months ago, *chère.* And I believe you know the answer to that question yourself."

Sky had been about to protest when Severin disappeared. No prelude, no fading out or possibility of it being a trick of the eye. One moment he was sitting facing Sky across the wooden table, the next he was not.

Then he was again.

Sky scrambled away from the little table, knocking over her cup of tea as she reached for the door. Only Severin's voice stopped her.

"Don't leave yet, sweetness. I was merely trying to answer your question as best I could. I'm a Pathfinder, and as they say, it takes one to know one. And it's also one very good reason why I'd never dream of harming you."

What she had just witnessed wasn't possible, was against the laws of physics.

But it's no more impossible than what you've done yourself, her internal voice countered. She had, in fact, done exactly what Severin had just demonstrated, only with a three-month intermission, and con-siderably less panache.

"How—how did you do that?"

Severin laughed. "The same way you do it, *chère*. I focus on a choice, trace the pathways which unfold from it." He traced a pattern with one finger on the table, like a tree trunk with branches stemming off in all directions. "Those strands of light, you know? They are the pathways. Then I concentrate on the pathway I want, until—*poof!*—it bursts open and I'm there, in another version of now." His finger skipped across the polished wood tabletop as though jumping from one branch of the tree to another.

Sky returned to her seat silently, trying to fathom what he was telling her. "You just go to an alternate reality? Then come back whenever you want?"

Severin stubbed out his cheroot, not looking at her for what seemed like the first time in hours. She had the odd sensation that something was missing, as though having his attention was somehow necessary.

"Of course."

"How do you control it?"

His eyes met hers again, pure cerulean blue. "At first, I had to practice, as it seems you will have to. It's like playing chess—once you see all the pieces, know how they move, all the strategies, the dependencies, then you can see the path that'll get you to where you want to be. Checkmate."

Sky had seen TV shows about conmen who could slick-talk their way in and out of almost anything. Had she given some sign that told him she played chess?

"Don't give me those eyes. Chess was an easy call—the game is a scaled-down version of what we do. We are exceptional players." Severin leaned sideways and swung his legs onto the bench seat, crossing them at the ankles.

"You're good at reading people, though, aren't you? That's just you, not a trait of . . . our kind?"

"Perhaps." Severin smiled through a cloud of smoke. "I knew as soon as I saw you spill out from under the stands that you were new to pathfinding." He tilted his head to one side, curious. "How did you die?"

Sky's heart beat an erratic rhythm. "What do you mean?"

"A Pathfinder's gift is only triggered when one version of himself—or *herself*—is about to die. It's been that way ever since the first Pathfinder accidentally materialized inside a tree : . . but that's another story. For me, I died defending something important to me. Or would have, had I not switched out with another version of myself just as the killing blow landed." His fingers twitched. "I spent a week in that other Severin's life before I realized it was not my own. When I was finally pulled back to my own life, I found myself tethered to the man who had killed that other version of me."

Severin's quick fingers had lit another cheroot before he continued. "The decision to take back what was mine was what made me a true Pathfinder. That decision, and the item I'd been willing to die for, anchor me to my own life so that I can never get lost.

Without an anchor, I would be cast adrift. It's just unfortunate my anchor resides in that murderous bastard's pocket." He took a long draw on his cheroot, and Sky gagged as he released it into the small space.

"What is it, though? Your anchor?"

"Some would call it a fairy tale, but it was something my father handed down to me, like his father before him. But tell me, how can you know so little about your gift, *chère*? Did your parents never teach you?"

"I don't think they know what I can do," Sky said.

Severin shook his head. "That's not possible. It's always passed down the bloodline."

Maybe Mom or Dad can do what I do, Sky thought. She dismissed the idea almost immediately. If they could, it should have occurred to them that that's where she had disappeared to when she died. And if it hadn't at the time, surely it would have when she showed up again three months later. There was no way they would have left her thinking she was going crazy if they could explain what was really going on.

They wouldn't. No way.

"Are there many of us? These . . . Pathfinders?"

"Very few, I'm afraid. We tend to attract attention, being as we're not quite *of this world.* People stare, not knowing why they stare, but knowing that they covet. You follow?" Sky looked at him blankly and Severin's mouth curled up at one corner. "You've never noticed how folks shove each other out of the way just to be near you? How you're never alone for long because someone always wants to be wherever you are? How even animals are drawn to you?"

"Oh yeah. I didn't realize you meant *that.*"

Severin laughed, but the sound tapered off as his expression grew serious. "Many will destroy what they covet if they cannot have it. Then there are others, people who are drawn to your power because they feed on it like parasites. People like Gage."

Sky stared at the man who had started talking in riddles around his cheroot.

"*Sky!*"

She turned to peer through the grimy window of the trailer at the sound of Jared's voice, but there was no sign of him.

"Aside from my parents, who were both gifted, you are the first I have met."

Sky shifted in her seat. Something didn't feel right, and it was more than just the general unfamiliarity of sitting in a tiny, smoke-filled circus trailer, sixteen years in the past, with a man who could travel between realities.

"*Help me, Sky!*"

There was no mistaking it this time. Jared's frightened voice was as clear as if he had yelled right in her ear, and Sky's heart started racing. *I need to get out of here.*

The pounding in her chest intensified as Sky felt that light-headedness take hold. The air seemed to charge around her, to snap with the promise of lightning.

"You're leaving so soon, *chère?* Do come back again, won't you?"

Severin's voice grew distant, but his eyes and his smile were clear as day until the moment Sky was thrust into a strange place, alone and in darkness.

❧ 17 ❧

"JARED?"

Sky whispered his name, feeling cold grass beneath her feet. Jared didn't answer. Her eyes adjusted to the crisp moonlight after a few seconds, and she saw that she was standing next to the wooden siding of the Vega house.

Oh crap.

A glance upward told her that it was late, as none of the windows showed any light. Not even Sean's window on the ground floor, which she would have to sneak past to leave the property.

But Sky knew she couldn't just go home. The panic in Jared's voice had been very real, even if Sky had no idea how he had followed her into the past, or where he had disappeared to in the circus thoroughfare. When he'd called her name, he'd made Sky believe he needed her, and he needed her *now*.

That meant she had only one choice: she would have to go back into the woods to find him, assuming he was somewhere near his van. If he wasn't . . . well, Sky hadn't a clue where to look.

But her bare toes were already going numb from standing on the cold grass, not to mention the gooseflesh covering the rest of her. It would take her at least a half hour and some fairly impressive sneaking to go home, grab some clothes and shoes, and run all the way to the entrance to the woods.

Too long.

Sky had another option. She didn't feel good about it, but it was looking like the only choice if she didn't want to lose time or toes getting to Jared.

Sky ducked low as she crept past Sean's bedroom window, then around to the other side of the house where the old shed stood with its door shut, but—as Sky knew from experience—not locked. Wary of the creaking hinges, she inched the door open just enough that she could grab Officer Vega's raggedy gardening boots, and slip back out again.

Sky shivered. There was no convenient jacket in the shed, and she couldn't afford the delay to go home for her coat. She would just have to run.

The moon was a silvery spotlight marking her journey past the Swiveller household, along Provencher Street and to the iron gate at the entrance to the woods.

It was at this point that Sky began cursing. She kept cursing until the sound of someone laughing behind her made her whirl around.

"Sean?"

He chewed his lip like it was all that was keeping him from doubling over. Then he shrugged off his jacket.

"I've never heard you swear like that before," he said, wrapping the duffle coat around her. It was still warm from his skin.

Sean stepped past her to the iron railings she had so recently called several ugly names and worked the metal jack between them.

"I'm going to overlook that you passed right by my window and didn't ask me to come with you on whatever crazy mission we're on this time," he continued winding the handle on the jack, and the space between the bars increased, "and just assume you have no objection to me following you up here to lend a hand."

Sky leaned over his hunched back and hugged him as tightly as she could. "You're very awesome like that. But we really need to hurry." After Sean gave her an inquiring look, Sky tried to come up with a brief explanation for what they were doing and failed. "I'll tell you all about it later, but for now we need to run."

⁂

THEY SMELLED THE smoke first. The first flicker of fire came into view just as they neared the clearing. It hadn't spread beyond the van, but the ground around it was already charred and barren.

"Oh my god!" Sky shouted as something shattered inside the van, and she and Sean sprinted through the trees toward it. "Do you think Jared's in there?"

Sky's breath came hard and fast, her heart thumping in her chest. Sean didn't answer.

The heat intensified as they reached the van. Shielding her face with her arm, Sky edged toward the van's door. She pulled her sleeve down over her hand and tried the handle. The metal burned even through the fabric, and Sky yanked her hand away.

The van door slid open on its tracks, the sudden intake of oxygen rushing the flames out—straight at Sean.

"Sean!"

But before Sky could move toward him, he'd dodged to the side, the fire spitting out into the night before retreating. Bright dots danced in front of Sky's eyes, but she still saw something dark inside the van. Sean caught her as she tried to get past him.

"Let me," he said, and leaped through the doorway.

The air rushing with him drew the fire up in an angry wall. Sky screamed. She tried to get nearer, but the heat was unbearable.

"Sean!" Sky had only taken one step toward the fire when a cool hand grabbed her arm.

"Get back, girl. He may not have meant to start it, but the flames will rise if he panics. That boy's got his mother's fire." Madame Curio's bony elbow dug into Sky's ribs and she stumbled backward. The old woman brought up the black nozzle of the fire extinguisher and let fly a gush of white foam. "I knew this thing would come in handy after last time."

"Last time? You mean when the circus burned?"

Madame Curio glanced at Sky, but didn't answer. After a few more seconds of dousing the fire, the drenched figures of Sean and

Jared emerged, with Jared draped over Sean in something between a fireman's lift and a human cape.

The two landed heavily at Sky's feet. Sean coughed and sputtered, black smears around his nose and lips where he'd breathed in the dirty smoke.

Sky wiped at the dark smears on his face, clenching her jaws to keep from bawling. Sean smiled and caught her hand, even as he continued coughing.

"I'm fine," he said his voice raspy. "Couldn't wake Jared."

Sky was shocked at how deathly pale Jared looked in the fire's dying orange glow. "Jared?" She shook him by the shoulders. "JARED!"

He heaved in a breath, eyes opening wide. Then he, too, started coughing, until he finally hacked up the contents of his stomach.

Sky wrapped her arms around Sean, hoping he wouldn't notice her hot tears on his neck.

"Where did he go?" Sean said next to her ear.

Sky peered all around them. Jared had disappeared, leaving no trace of himself except for the mess in the grass.

"Madame Curio's gone, too," Sky said. "Where did she go? And did you hear what she said about Jared having his mother's fire?"

The van was completely dark, though curls of steam still rose from the metal roof. The fire extinguisher lay abandoned just outside the still open van door, but its owner was nowhere to be seen.

The heavy weight of Sean buckling in a coughing fit against her brought Sky back to the moment. It didn't matter where Jared and Madame Curio had disappeared to. "We need to get you to a hospital."

Sean shook his head. "How would we explain all this? The fire's out now, Jared's vanished, and all we have left is a burned-out van in the middle of the already burned woods. I'll be fine, I just need to get home."

Sky studied him for a moment. "You promise you're okay?"

He flashed his brilliant smile at her and twined his sooty fingers through hers. "Promise."

"Good." Sky punched him not too gently in the shoulder.

"What was that for?"

"Jumping into burning vans and scaring the crap out of me!"

Sean laughed, then started coughing again. "Fine. The next burning van we come across that needs jumping into, it's all yours. Now let's get home, the sun will be up in . . . well, still another six hours or so. But still, it's late."

They walked back through the woods much more slowly than they'd entered. Sky's whole body felt like it was made of lead. Still, she watched out for any sign of Jared or the old woman.

Finally they reached the gap in the fence and crawled through, following their own footsteps through the grass, back down the hill and along Provencher Street until they came to Sky's house. It was all in darkness, and Sky looked wearily at the trellis she needed to climb back up to her bedroom.

"Need a boost?" Sean whispered, his hands already hovering at her waist. Sky turned in his hold.

"You could have been really badly hurt because of me," she said finally.

"Hey, this wasn't your fault. And if we hadn't been there, Jared could've died tonight. Besides, I'm fine. Or at least I will be once I've washed off this smoke-stink." Sean sniffed himself and grimaced.

"Sean . . . I didn't tell you how I knew Jared needed my help."

He looked at her warily. "You didn't."

"I went back again, and I think I took Jared with me somehow."

"Back?"

"To the circus. To the past. I met this guy called Severin. He was the ringmaster in the circus that was here, I think. He's . . . he's like me. He can do what I do, and he was telling me how it works, but then when we were talking, Jared disappeared, and I heard him shouting for me like he was far away. Do you think maybe I did something that left him like that, unconscious with his van burning around him?"

Sean's hands moved from where he'd been stroking his thumbs along her jaw and cupped her face while he kissed her, just once. "You'd never hurt anyone, Sky—intentionally or otherwise. I know we don't *know* what's happening to you, but it does seem like something that only affects you. I can't see how you could have done anything to leave Jared in trouble like that. But it is something I'd like to ask the guy about." He kissed her again, a quick brush of lips. "Sorry, I know I must taste like bonfire. Now let's get you up onto that balcony before your dad catches us and crushes me like a bug."

It was much harder climbing onto her balcony than usual, and whether it was her fatigue or her reluctance to leave Sean, she couldn't tell. In any case, she stood watching his figure disappear into the night for a long moment before she went inside.

Her hand was already reaching for the doorknob when she saw the note taped to the glass door panel in front of her. Even in the light of the moon, the large print was easy to read.

HE'S COME BACK FOR YOU, PATHFINDER.
STAY AWAY FROM HIM OR YOU WILL
REGRET IT.

❧ 18 ❧

"SKYLAR."

A sound like a growl escaped her, but she clamped her teeth shut on it. She kept hearing his voice in her head, over and over.

"I need your help."

Sky heard Jared calling for her, a note of fear and pain in his voice that set her heart thudding against her ribs. Sky stuffed her head under the pillow but didn't dare make a sound, not even into the muffling fiber of the mattress. The Blood House heard everything, and one couldn't always tell which sounds it would carry to wake sleeping parents down the hall.

"For God's sake, I'm outside! Can you come to the window?"

Sky held her breath, not moving a muscle. Had his voice actually been outside, or was she now imagining things as well? It hadn't sounded like it had been outside, and if it had been, her parents would have heard it, too.

"You're not imagining things. Open the freaking window and you'll see."

Slowly, she slid out of bed, grabbed her robe, and opened the curtains. For a moment, she couldn't see anything through the condensation covering the glass. Then there he was.

Sky saw the outline of a man standing on the balcony just beyond the doors and stepped back, breath catching in her throat.

Just like I saw that night outside the kitchen window, the first time I traveled back.

He leaned closer, his silvery eyes lost in shadow. Then he stuck out his tongue.

"It'll stick to the window," Sky whispered, giggling as he moved to stand straight and discovered that that was exactly what had happened. It came unstuck with a sticky sound, and Jared winced.

Sky turned the key in the lock carefully, easing the doors open. Rather than letting Jared move past her into the room, she stepped outside, her toes curling at how cold the night had become.

"What are you doing here? And were you talking to me just now? I'm amazed my folks didn't hear you."

Jared was poking tentatively at his frost-burned tongue with one finger, but he still managed to sigh. He shifted his weight and shuddered like it had caused him pain. "My leg got cut up getting out of my van. Do you think you could take a look at it? All my first-aid stuff, it just went up in smoke. And I can't afford a hospital."

Now that her eyes had adjusted to the moonlight, she could see a dark stain spreading outward on the lower leg of his jeans. It could only be blood, and it looked like there was a lot of it.

"Come inside, but be quiet," she whispered, turning to find that the french windows had closed noiselessly behind her.

The Blood House isn't too sure about Jared, then.

Sky turned the handle and pushed against it—not roughly, as the window was likely to fly open and crash against the wall—but with enough determination that it had no choice but to swing inward and allow them both inside. She ushered Jared into her small bathroom and closed the door. After the dim light outside, the bulb overhead left them both squinting.

Jared leaned back against the sink and bent to try to pull the blood-soaked denim up his leg.

"Damn skinny jeans. I'll have to take them off."

Sky turned from where she had been rummaging in the cabinet for first-aid supplies and almost dropped everything as she caught him undoing the zipper on his pants. Jared pulled the denim past his knees with a grimace, exposing a nasty gash across his right shin. "I didn't even feel it at the time," he said, touching the raw skin around it gingerly. "Hurts like hell now, though."

Sky knelt in front of him to inspect the dark specks she could see in the wound. "Looks like you've got soot in it. I'll have to clean it properly before I bandage it."

Jared stayed still while Sky worked, only wincing slightly as she cleaned the cut with antiseptic spray. She reached up for the gauze she'd given Jared to hold and he handed it over.

"Thank you for doing this, Sky."

She looked up from her position on the bathroom tiles in front of him, studiously avoiding looking at anything between his bandaged shin and his face.

"Are you going to tell me what the hell that voice trick was you did just now? And what happened when we went back to the circus? Where did you go?"

Jared sighed. "I didn't actually *go* anywhere. That's kind of the problem."

Sky finished tying the ends of the bandage around his leg while she waited for him to continue.

"I didn't actually travel back with you, Sky. I was just a passenger, seeing it through your eyes. That's what I do, I get into people's heads. Because you went back, my mind, or whatever you call it, went back with you."

Was that why Madame Curio didn't seem to see him? And what she meant by there being a "worm" in my head?

Jared nodded as though she had spoken aloud. "Yes, exactly. You could see my astral form, but nobody else could. When the fire started back here, where my body was still stuck in my van, I got catapulted back into it. But the smoke was choking me up pretty bad and I must have passed out before I could get outta there. I'm just glad you heard me call for help, 'cuz I was too out of it by that point to try and get into the mind of anyone else. It takes a lot of effort, and doesn't always work."

Again, Sky busied herself with putting away her medical supplies and avoided looking at him.

"Aren't you going to say anything?"

She closed the lid on the first-aid kit before finally turning her face up to him. "I'm just trying to figure out whether you're somehow playing an elaborate prank on me, or if I'm going nuts."

"You don't believe me?"

She sighed. "Look, I want to, but what you're saying just isn't possible. Weird things happen here all the time. We have a haunted weathervane, for goodness' sake. But everyone knows that if you look closely enough, you'll come up with a reasonable explanation. Maybe the school's situated in a spot which is prone to little tornadoes, and that makes it spin like crazy sometimes. Or maybe someone's rigged a turning mechanism onto the roof. Whatever, it doesn't matter. It's just one weird thing that just *is* because it's in Blackfin. And people just accept it, go 'huh,' and move on. But you—you're claiming to have some magical power that lets you inside people's heads."

"It's not magical. It's just something I can do that other people can't, like some people have an instinct for languages or can read maps or feel when it's about to rain. I get inside people's heads. How else do you think I could call out to you from the balcony without your parents hearing me? And how do you explain what *you* can do?"

"I—"

The door handle turned, silencing them both instantly.

"*Coco*, what are you . . ."

Jared hastily pulled his jeans up as Gui's face appeared in the doorway, one eyebrow scrunched up where he had obviously been sleeping on it. It only added to his confused expression. That quickly changed, though, as his features morphed into a mask of anger. It was almost a contradiction to his low, even tone.

"Jared, what are you doing in my house?"

Jared looked up from fastening the button at the waistband of his jeans. "I know this looks bad, but it's not what you think."

"Skylar, get up off the floor."

Sky stood, realizing exactly what it *had* looked like. She felt the blood rush to her face. "Dad! I was just taking a look at his—"

Gui scrunched his eyes shut. "Hush, Skylar. Jared, get out. And be quiet—I don't want my wife to hear you." Sky noticed how his fists were clenched at his sides as Jared squeezed past him through the bathroom doorway and slipped out the open french doors. "And you—go to bed. We will speak of this in the morning."

"But Dad . . ."

"Go to bed, Skylar." He walked out, muttering under his breath in French. For once, Sky was glad he'd never taught her to speak his native language.

THEY DID NOT speak of it in the morning. In fact, Gui did not speak at all, passing only silent looks of disapproval over their Sunday pancakes until Sky finally gave up trying to outlast his disappointment. Sky had grabbed the note from her nightstand on her way downstairs, thinking she would show it to her father. But with the sour mood still furrowing his brow, she knew it wasn't the time to mention it. The letter remained a crinkly secret in her pocket.

"Nothing happened between me and Jared."

Gui chewed a mouthful of pancakes slowly. Then he sipped his coffee—also slowly—before finally breaking his silence. "I know that, *coco*. That does not mean I can just pat you on the head like a good little girl when I find you sneaking around with a half-clothed boy."

"Wait, you *know* nothing happened between me and Jared?" Gui didn't nod, but his eyes met hers in acknowledgment. "How?"

"You are not the kind of girl who can like one boy and do things with another boy."

Sky blushed at her father's knowing look. At least one of her parents had noticed her feelings for Sean, and it was just as well it was not her mother. Sky allowed herself a small smile.

"Does this mean I'm not grounded?"

Gui laughed. "It does not."

"But Dad—"

Her father silenced her by holding up one finger. "You are grounded for this weekend for giving your papa a heart attack." He sipped his coffee thoughtfully. "Oh, and you are *never* allowed to have a boy alone in your room. Not until I am dead and buried."

⁂

BEING GROUNDED WAS oddly comforting—especially since Gui's definition of *grounded* meant taking Sky to watch a movie in Oakridge and picking up takeout from the diner on their way home.

That had not given Sky an opportunity to do anything about the note. She didn't want to blacken Gui's mood again by showing him what could only be interpreted as a threat. But maybe her friends could help her figure it out—when Gui finally ungrounded her.

After all, the note was *real*, something even Bo couldn't just roll her eyes at, and she desperately wanted their help unraveling the mysteries, which just seemed to be getting more and more tangled around her.

Her phone beeped, and she realized her father hadn't remembered to confiscate it. She dived across the bed to retrieve it from the nightstand. The message was from Bo.

Party in the woods tonight. Pick you up at 10.

Sky groaned. Can't, grounded. The woods??

Bo: Yep. Still avoiding me?

Sky: WTH? I'm not avoiding you.

Bo: You're so lame.

Sky could practically hear Bo's sigh. But they were going to the woods, and might stumble across Madame Curio or the circus or Jared's burned-out van. That couldn't be a good thing.

Thirty seconds later her phone beeped again. This time it was Cam. *Bo says you're not coming!!! WHY???*

Sky: Grounded. Long story.

Cam: SNEAK OUT!!!

Sky eyed the french windows. She really should do something to try to keep her classmates out of the woods, but she didn't want to go against her father's wishes. Not *really*.

As she watched, the latch clicked open and the doors slowly and soundlessly swung inward.

"You think it's a good idea, huh?" Sky felt silly addressing the house, but she was quite willing to accept any advocate to the scheme. "I hope you've got my back when my parents catch me, then."

❧ 19 ❧

SHE WAITED AN eternity for her parents to go to bed, although their bedtime was only ten thirty. By ten forty-five, she could hear nothing from their room.

That was not a good sign. Unless her mother was snoring, that generally meant she was still awake. Sky crept along the hallway toward her parents' room to check. She had stayed in her clothes, slipping her coat on over them in preparation for a quick departure, the anonymous note tucked carefully in her pocket. But her boots stayed in her hand for the moment.

The Blood House silenced the floorboards for her, allowing her to sneak in her socked feet to listen at the door. She heard nothing at first, but kept waiting, just to be sure.

"Leave him, we . . . she mustn't know . . ."

Sky froze, but her mother's voice had a muffled quality only achieved in sleep. She turned to creep back to her room when another sound stopped her.

"NO, GAGE! DON'T!"

The gasping of her mother waking in fright was followed by her father's baritone, shushing her to calm down, telling her that it had all been a nightmare. But Sky had heard her mother utter the word *Gage*. She didn't know who he was, but remembered what Madame Curio had said about Jared the second time Sky visited her in the woods—that Jared belonged to Gage.

Who is *he?*

That nagging doubt that Sky had been trying to ignore about Jared solidified into something she couldn't ignore. She was already heading back to her room when her stomach plummeted, and the walls of the hallway fell away in a shower of bright light, sparks turning to ribbons, until one burst open and consumed her.

⚜

CRATES AND EQUIPMENT and the chirruping of bells somewhere nearby surrounded her. A mix of sawdust and grass blades prickled her feet through her socks. Sky leaned against a crate and bent to tie her boots.

Though she heard the now familiar sounds of the circus nearby, this tent smelled different from the Big Top. It was musty, a mix of old wood and animal fur, and it felt colder without the press of bodies lining the stands.

Sky felt a crawling sensation at the back of her neck. She wasn't alone.

Sky whirled around and met the bared yellow fangs of an enormous wolf. She jerked backward, landing hard against a large wooden crate behind her.

There was a clash of teeth and claws against metal, and she saw that the wolves—three in all, great white beasts with sallow fur and teeth as long as her fingers—were hurling themselves against the inside of their cage to try to reach her.

She forced in a shaky breath, rubbing her arm where she had jarred it against the crate.

The sound of footsteps had Sky ducking down next to the crate. She edged around it, keeping out of view as footsteps entered the tent where she was hiding. The paper in her pocket crackled as she shifted her position, and she edged it out slowly so it wouldn't give her away.

"They're your animals. Why would I know what ails them?"

The lazy drawl was definitely Severin's. She peeked around the corner of the crate to try and see who he was with, but the movement brought her closer to the wolves, and they leaped again.

Whoever Severin was with gave no audible reply. "Fine, I'll see to them."

Severin's quick, light footsteps brought him right to where Sky crouched. Slowly, she looked up. But he didn't appear to have noticed her, despite almost standing on her toe.

"They must be hungry. Gui usually feeds them." At Sky's sharp intake of breath, Severin glanced down, the shake of his head almost imperceptible.

The wolves calmed as Severin placed himself between Sky and their cage.

"I'll see that it's done, Gage."

Gage!

The other made no sound whatsoever before his footsteps approached Sky's hiding place. One look at Severin's face told her she was about to be discovered.

Oh crud.

Her heart was already jack-hammering from seeing the wolves, but now she thought it might burst from her chest.

"I said I'd see to it." His tone remained lazy, but the jab of his booted toe at her hip was not.

The footsteps stopped inches away from where she crouched, just as the floating sensation took hold of her. She focused on it until sparks filled her peripheral vision, the pathways becoming clear. A sharp sliver of light behind her eyelids pointed the way back to her own time, her own home, and she felt something pulling her toward it.

But not quickly enough. The wolves had begun whining and yelping inside the cage. The man leaned over them and Sky cringed back against the crate, trying to make herself invisible behind Severin's legs.

And as the man snapped his gaze to her, she had a moment to recognize his dark, piercing eyes and chalk-white face before the note slipped from her fingers, and she vanished.

SKY'S HEART HAMMERED her brain back to wakefulness.

She knew it had to be the same man her mother was dreaming about, the same face that Sky saw at the circus and the ice rink and in the newspaper clipping in the attic. But what did Gage want with her? And what did Jared have to do with him?

Both her feet had gone numb inside her boots. She wiggled them off and kicked them out from under the comforter, letting them fall to the floor with a dull *thud*. Except the thud was not as dull as it should have been had they landed on her bedroom carpet.

Not my room.

Sky went rigid as she realized someone else was lying in the bed next to her.

"Uh, Sky, did you take a wrong turn?"

Sky recognized the whispered voice, but that only made her heart race faster.

In the barest light filtering around the curtains in Sean's room, she saw the outline of his head on the pillow next to her, his hair mussed from sleep and his eyes as round and wide as hers felt.

"Uh, yeah."

Sean shifted, the groan of bedsprings now sounding like exploding mortar shells in the silence of the house, where Officer Holly

Vega was no doubt unholstering her weapon to come downstairs and shoot the intruder.

"It's two thirty in the morning."

Sky's mouth went dry. Almost four hours had passed, but she hadn't been at the circus for more than five minutes.

"Have I been here long?" she whispered back.

"I'm not sure. Something woke me a moment ago. Sounded like something fell onto the floor."

Sky still didn't move, now growing uncomfortably hot. She was in Sean's bed, in the middle of the night—uninvited.

"I'm sorry, I don't know how I ended up here. I'll go—"

He caught her wrist just as she was about to throw back the comforter.

"Go where? There's no way you'll be able to sneak out without Aunt Holly catching you."

Sky paused. If the policewoman caught her, what possible excuse could she give that wouldn't look suspicious? None.

"But I can't stay here."

"You can. I mean, if that's all right with you. Stay."

"Oh." Sky forced her muscles to relax a little. "But what if your aunt comes in?"

A brush of Sean's fingers against hers had Sky squeezing his hand in reflex.

"She never comes in here without knocking, and even then,

rarely. She gets up at six sharp, then gets showered and dressed and knocks on my door to ask if I want breakfast at six twenty-five. If you can sneak out while she's in the shower, there won't be any chance of her hearing you."

"What about Cam?"

Sean's fingers flexed. "She stayed at Bo's house after the party last night. She's been staying there a lot since . . . you know."

Sky's heart did a flip. Her friends were still feeling the effects of her disappearance, even if she hadn't actually died like they thought.

"Did they find anything at the woods? Was Madame Curio still there? What did she say?"

Sean shushed her when her voice crept above a whisper. They both stayed quiet for a minute, waiting for the sound of Sean's aunt coming downstairs. When no telltale creak of floorboards gave away her approach, Sean relaxed again next to her.

Sky scooted closer to Sean to whisper. He leaned in, bringing them close enough that she could feel the heat of his skin on her lips.

She held her breath. Sean was either a lot less nervous about the position they were in, or he was hiding it very well.

"Jared had already fixed it so that nobody could get past the gate. He'd even put vandal grease on the fence. The party moved down to the beach, but it didn't go on for very long. Nobody really seemed in the mood."

At least one thing had gone in Sky's favor.

"Are you sure you don't mind if I stay here? I can sleep on the floor."

Sean's answer was to wrap his arm across her waist, rolling her so that her back was to his chest.

"Good night, Sky."

✤ 20 ✤

SKY KNEW SOMETHING was wrong even before opening her eyes. When she did, the stern figure of Officer Holly Vega loomed in the doorway.

Sean remained asleep, snoring softly with his face to the wall.

Officer Vega made a series of hand gestures, conveying that she would be waiting in the kitchen for Sky to join her there.

Sky nodded, mortified.

Sky spidered her way out of Sean's bed, pausing to tie on her boots—as though that might make things seem more appropriate to Sean's aunt—and looked at his sleeping face. He looked younger, somehow, a frown creasing his forehead. Sky tucked away her smile and crept from the room.

She steeled herself and sat down opposite the police officer at her dark wood dining table. Officer Vega slid a steaming cup of coffee across the table to Sky.

"We might be having a slightly different conversation had I not seen that you were fully clothed in my nephew's bed, but Sean has a right to his privacy and so do you. So let's just not go there." Officer Vega paused before continuing, "But I am *not* happy to find unexpected visitors in my house. I could have shot you, Skylar, and

I'd really rather not have to refile all the paperwork I did when you died the last time." She smiled thinly. "So if you're staying over, I want to know you're here. Stick a note on Sean's door, hang a sock from the door handle—*whatever*—just so that I know. Are we clear?"

Sky nodded. "I'm sorry if finding me there was weird."

Officer Vega laughed. "I wouldn't have known you were there at all if you didn't talk in your sleep. I'll be having this same conversation with Sean when he wakes up, but I wanted to speak with you alone first. I thought I should update you on the investigation."

Sky almost scalded herself with coffee. "Investigation?"

"After the Swivellers' assault on you last week, I took a look around the property—unofficially, at first—to see if I could unearth some connection between that and what happened on your birthday."

Officer Vega waited for Sky to connect the dots.

"You thought they might have been the ones who pushed me off the pier?"

The police officer tipped her head to one side. "Possibly. But either way, after they admitted digging up your grave to bury their dog"—her mouth twisted in a grimace—"I knew they would be able to answer a few questions which have been bothering me ever since you came back."

"Oh?"

"Like what happened to the body buried in your place after they unearthed it. And who it belonged to, if not to you. After all, it wasn't inconceivable that a body might have washed up on the beach from outside Blackfin." She stood and walked into the family room, only to reappear a moment later holding a manila folder. "But then I found these hidden in the old barn behind the Swivellers' place." She put the folder on the table in front of Sky, but kept her hand on top of it for a moment. "I must warn you, there are photos in there that are very disturbing. If you'd rather not look at them, I completely understand, but I don't see how you'll believe what's in them otherwise."

Officer Vega slid her hand from the folder and went back to her seat opposite Sky.

There was no way she wanted to see whatever was in those photos if the steady, practical woman facing her called them "disturbing" and was now looking at her in silent apology. But a part of Sky knew she *had* to.

Her fingers trembled as she opened the folder.

"Oh God . . . are these . . . are these pictures of *me*?"

The photos showed a girl uncannily similar to Sky, except for one tiny detail: she was dead. There was no doubt about her unfortunate state, her eyes shriveled and sunken behind her closed eyelids, her skin blanched a terrible shade of white. Almost as disturbing was the way the girl had been posed, sitting on a hay bale in what had to be the Swivellers' barn. Sky didn't recognize the dress she was wearing, but it was a baggy, floral number that she suspected had gone missing from Mrs. Swiveller's closet.

"There was no sign of the body, and I couldn't get the boys to confess what they'd done with it. All I found were these photos."

"Why did you show them to me?"

Sky glared at the older woman.

"I'm sorry I had to do that, but I needed to be certain. The girl *is* you, unless you have an identical twin I've never heard about. Still, you've maintained since you reappeared that you had no idea you've been missing—presumed dead—for the last three months. And then I find these photos, with you most certainly in them, and I had to ask myself, is the girl in these photos really dead, or just playing some twisted kind of dress-up? Has this whole thing been a prank gone too far?"

Officer Vega silenced Sky's protest by taking her hand.

"Skylar, it was the only *logical* explanation I could think of. I know it's not something you would do, but I wouldn't be doing my job if I didn't rule out every possibility. You understand, don't you?"

Sky forced her jaw to unclench. "I suppose so."

Officer Vega leaned back, spreading her hands. "So that's what I've got: a metric ton of unanswered questions, with no logical explanation."

Sky studied the photos in front of her again, debating over telling the policewoman about the lost note. But that would mean having to explain what exactly a Pathfinder was, and Sky wasn't sure how to explain it herself. "By logical, I take it you mean within the usual laws of physics?"

Officer Vega's eyes narrowed. "Anything beyond that is outside of my scope, I'm afraid."

Sky's problem wasn't a matter for the police, and it looked like Officer Vega had enough to deal with in figuring out who the missing corpse had been. Except Sky knew who the corpse had been—herself, only from another version of her life, displaced from her own reality to die in this one. But the body hadn't been pulled back to its own reality the way she had.

Is that because that *Skylar Rousseau wasn't a Pathfinder, or because she was dead?*

She clamped her mouth shut to stop the sob she could feel trying to escape her.

How can I feel guilty about killing someone—someone who's basically me—when I didn't even know I'd done it?

But she did. And there was nothing she could do to make it better. But there was one thing the police officer might be able to help her with.

"Officer Vega, do you know anything about a man called Gage?"

The woman shook her head. "Why do you ask?"

How could Sky explain the strange feeling she had that he wanted something from her, when she'd never actually spoken to the man? And did he even exist in this reality, or was he tied to the circus, sixteen years in the past? "Never mind, just thinking out loud. So what do you suggest I do?"

Officer Vega flipped the manila folder shut. "Same as I suggested before. If you want answers, talk to your mother." The older woman smiled. "Do you remember the first time I met you and your mother, Skylar?" Sky shook her head. "No, of course not. You were only about three years old at the time. But she told me she was sorry to hear about my husband passing away."

Sky didn't understand the significance.

"Nobody here knew about that. I'd made it a condition of the transfer. A woman cop—the only cop in a small town—has a hard enough time building a rapport with the locals as it is. If everyone here had known I'd only left New York after Barney was shot, they'd have treated me differently. I didn't want pity, Sky. I just wanted to do my job. So I didn't tell anyone, not a soul."

"But Mom knew," Sky said, unease settling into resolve.

Officer Vega nodded, that knowing smile still in place. "Your mom knew."

※≈◎≤※

AFTER SCHOOL, SKY found her mother on the back porch at the Blood House, a thick blanket around her as she rocked back and forth on the old swing.

"You knew where I'd gone for those three months, didn't you, Mom?"

Lily Rousseau looked up at her daughter with bloodshot eyes. She looked so unlike herself in that moment, Sky wondered whether she had accidentally traveled to another version of her life where her mom was a drunk. But Lily was the same Lily that Sky had always known—just one who had secrets keeping her awake at night, and a daughter she was lying to.

"I didn't know at the time, no. I thought you'd died, and I didn't know it happened that way—that another you would be left here in your place." Tears slid down her cold pink cheeks, and she swiped at them briskly. "I still see her, Skylar. It still feels *in here*"— she held her hand to her chest—"like my baby died. But she wasn't you, and then I feel guilty for mourning a child who wasn't really mine." She sniffled, still looking furious.

"Why haven't you said anything?"

"Because I'm your mother, and it's my job to carry these things inside so you don't have to." Her eyes met Sky's. "Hasn't helped though, has it?"

Sky climbed the back porch steps and sat down next to her mother. "Are you a Pathfinder, or is Dad?" Lily just shook her head, but something in her expression gave Sky the clue she'd been trying to ignore since she'd spoken to Severin. "Dad's not my real dad, is he?" Again, her mother shook her head, and Sky's heart broke. Her father had always been her rock, the one she could turn to when anything was bothering her, the one who could make her day brighter with a smile and hot chocolate.

"Do I even need to ask who my real father is?" Of course it had to be Severin. She had seen her pregnant mother at the circus, and

Severin himself had said he'd never met another Pathfinder except for his own parents.

"Severin refused to leave Gage, so I couldn't tell him about you. Gui and I had been friends for years, ever since I'd joined the circus. He promised to help me escape, to get away from Gage. Gage was a terrible man, Skylar. He did shocking, awful things, things I've tried so hard to forget. He kidnapped so many children, babies even, and forced them to perform in the circus just to line his pockets, gathering more and more gifted people into the troupe as we traveled from town to town. And after the fire, after we got away from that life, your father and I stayed together. We've been happy."

Sky had to take a deep breath before asking her next question. "Do you love Dad?"

Her mother looked up at her, shocked. "Of course I do! What Severin and I had was nothing more than a fling, and it had burned out before I even knew about you. Gui is the love of my life, more important to me than anything in this world, except for you. He makes me feel safe, protected. Loved.

"It means a lot when it's not something you've been raised with. I'm glad you don't know what it's like to live without that feeling." Lily met her daughter's stare.

"Then why did he move out while I was . . . in that other place?" Swallowing didn't help this time, and Sky had to brush away a tear. Her mother unwrapped one side of the blanket and pulled it around Sky.

"Things were just . . . Gui was angry with me for not finding out what happened to you that night."

"What do you mean?"

Lily freed one of her hands from the blanket, holding it out in front of her like she was catching snowflakes.

"When I touch someone, I see things about them. The important things that mark a person—meeting your first love, being afraid of the dark as a child, seeing your own child being born. It happens sometimes with places as well. Churches can be overwhelming, filled with people's memories of the happiest days and the saddest days of their life." Lily glanced over her shoulder. "Or like this house, with what happened to your father's family." There was a groan of wood behind them, and the door creaked inward.

"What happened here?"

Lily flexed the fingers on her still outstretched hand. "How about I show you?" Sky knew she must have looked dubious, as Lily smiled. "If you knew what happened, how your father and I ended up here, it might help you to understand." She held her hand out to Sky, and the look she gave her daughter was almost pleading. "Understand *me*."

❧ 21 ❧

THERE WERE NO flashes of light, no sense of being pulled from her core into the vastness of the pathways. Seeing the past through Lily's eyes was not at all like pathfinding.

Sky was on the porch swing one moment, and the next she was hovering outside a circus trailer like a disembodied spirit.

Sky scanned the field around her, and noticed the grass had an odd gray tinge to it. The color leeched more and more from her surroundings the farther she looked from where she now hovered. Even the rear section of the trailer looked fuzzy and out of focus as though someone had drawn a picture of it but forgotten to add in lines.

Her mother's voice spoke from right next to her, but she couldn't see her form.

"This is the portrait of memory. Some parts fade over time, or weren't remembered correctly to begin with, so you have to make sense of this kind of patchwork of truth and things forgotten. It'll make more sense as we go along."

Sky flailed as the scene around her changed again, and she now hovered on the opposite side of the trailer, next to two teenagers who *looked* like her parents.

Sky's arm passed through the wooden siding of the trailer as she tried to steady herself. At least, her arm *would* have passed through it. Looking down at where her body should have been, Sky saw nothing.

"We aren't really here, Skylar," her mom's voice said in her ear, startling her. "None of this is real anymore; it's just a memory."

The teenage versions of her parents were talking very quickly to one another, like someone had accidentally hit fast-forward on the playback.

"I can't understand what they're saying," Sky whispered.

"Sure you can. You're just not *used* to using your brain at this speed."

Sky concentrated. Gradually, the conversation slowed to a speed where she could understand it.

"What am I seeing?"

"This is the first time I met your father. He'd already been in the circus seven years with Severin and Gage. Gage took him from his hometown in France—a little village called Belle Dame du Pont—when he was eleven years old."

Sky remembered what she'd read up in the attic. "I think I read about that in a newspaper cutting, but I couldn't really under-stand it since it was in French."

Her mother laughed next to her. "I wondered when the house would start pointing you in the right direction."

Sky continued watching the couple as her mother's voice narrated. It was kind of obvious to her now that the pair really didn't know each other, but it was just as clear that the teenage Gui didn't like Lily.

"It took a while for you two to become friends, then?"

"I wasn't a very nice girl when I met him. He made me want to be better."

No sooner had she spoken, then the scene shifted. Her parents were still before her, only this time her mother was tied to a slowly spinning target as the teenage Gui wound up his throwing arm. Sky almost screamed when the hatchet left his hand, went whistling past her not-there body, and sank harmlessly into the wooden board next to Lily's cheek.

"A while, yes." Her mother's voice held laughter as she spoke in Sky's ear. "He didn't want me to join the circus, but he'd had no choice in the matter himself. I left home because I was terribly unhappy there. I didn't find the happiness I'd been looking for here, either."

The scene shifted again, and Sky felt nauseous as she settled into a hover next to the striped tarpaulin of the Big Top.

Gui barged past, toward where Lily's past self stood talking with an upset-looking young couple.

"I recognize this one," Sky confessed. "I've been here before."

"Then you know that I was expecting you by this time," her mother confirmed. "Gui and I had been working together on our act for almost two years, but when he found out I was pregnant, he refused to let me take any part in the shows. Gage didn't know about the baby—you—but he made Gui suffer for our refusal."

Her mother's voice had dropped, becoming flat and lifeless. Sky never wanted to know what punishment someone could have inflicted on her dad if it made her mother sound that way. She shuddered, remembering Gage's piercing eyes staring at her from the shadows. Wanting something from her.

"But you got away, right? Before the fire?"

Their surroundings melted away until they hovered near one of the largest trailers, darkness enveloping them. Raised voices carried from inside the trailer, and Lily's past self peeked through the lit window. Inside, Sky could see the enormous figure of her father towering over the man she had only previously glimpsed: Gage. His hair was slicked back against his head, his face blanched white like a ghoul. And between him and Gui was Severin.

"This all came before that," Lily whispered next to Sky.

The voices inside the trailer rose. Only Gage was silent.

"If you let us leave, I can convince them not to go to the police! You could even get out of town before they have the chance!" Sky recognized Gui's voice.

"And lose one of our acts? And what could possibly compel us to let Lily go with you, hmm?"

Hearing Severin arguing with her father made Sky's heart race. There was something about Severin's voice, something which didn't sound right, as though it wasn't his at all. It was the voice of a serpent, the hand reaching up through dark water to grab your ankle and pull you down. It was the creaking of a floorboard when you were alone in the house.

"She wants to leave with me!" Sky could see the tension in Gui's muscles.

Severin looked up at Gui standing next to him, and he sounded like himself again. "She does?"

Gui nodded tightly, still staring at Gage.

"They saw me, Gage. They *recognized* me. Do you think they'll just forget about it? You know your tricks don't work forever. They'll remember, and they'll report you. *Unless you let us go.*"

Sky watched Gui take a step forward, shoving Severin over against the wall until he was crowding over Gage. But Gage seemed undaunted, playing with a glass paperweight like he was about to start juggling with it, the white cast of his face making him look like a waxwork.

"We will consider it," Severin said finally, as though he spoke for them both.

"Why doesn't Gage say anything?" Sky whispered to her mother.

"He never spoke. He used others to speak for him."

It made sense now, the way Gui shouted at the man when it was only Severin who answered.

"You don't have time to cook up some new scheme to wriggle out of the situation, Gage. They saw me. If I don't go to them and convince them not to go to the police right now, it will be too late. Even you can't escape if they get the FBI involved, which they will. It's a kidnapping case."

The way Gage puckered his mouth made his face appear even more pointed. Still, it was Severin who spoke for him, and his voice was quicksilver.

"You will have my answer by morning."

It was possible the conversation continued, but the young Lily ran from the window, and the memory faded before them.

Sky thought for a moment that she was back in the real world with her mom on the back porch, but the sky was too dark, the early spring flowers open too soon for it to be the present. Even in Blackfin, where sunset chose its own time to fall, it took more than a few minutes to darken completely.

"Mom?" she whispered into the darkness. A light flickered on inside the Blood House as her mother's voice answered.

"This was the same night as the argument we just saw. But this—this is the memory the Blood House has given me."

Sky was about to question her further when footsteps approached from behind them.

Gage strode up the path, a bowler hat set low over his face. Sky hovered around the side of the house to follow him, assuming he was on his way to knock on the front door.

Is he here to try to bribe my grandparents not to go to the police?

Then she remembered how this would end, how it had already ended. The real reason her home was called the Blood House.

Gage was not alone. Perched on his hip, his face shadowed by the brim of Gage's hat, was the small boy Sky had seen at the circus. The boy with those piercing eyes that seemed to know too much for a child so young.

"Who is that little boy?" Sky whispered.

For a moment, Sky didn't think her mother was going to answer. "That's Jani Schwarz's son, Jimmy. He was lost in the fire."

Miss Schwarz's son?

The slippery way Gage smiled at the child turned Sky's stomach. She'd had no idea Miss Schwarz had ever had a child, and the thought of him being killed in the fire made Sky shudder.

Instead of climbing the steps to the front door, Gage continued around to the far side of the house, where the picture window looked into the family room. Still hovering silently, Sky and Lily followed. By the time they reached Gage, he was grinning at the boy again, cocking his head to one side as though they were having some silent conversation.

"Gage was really mute?"

"Yes," Lily whispered next to Sky, as though even the memory of him frightened her. "But he never needed to speak to make himself heard."

Gage leaned away from the boy after a moment, and the child shook his head. Sky watched as Gage pouted mockingly at him, and the boy buried his face in his neck. Gage set the boy down roughly and strode up to the window. From his pocket, he took what looked at first like an orange ball. But then Sky saw the eye sockets, the eerie imitation of a skull etched into it.

"What is that?"

"Gage needed the amber skull to focus his power. I never saw him without that thing, not once."

The little boy made a shrill sound, and Sky saw him watching Gage with his dark eyes wide in horror. But the moment Gage looked inside, the windows darkened until they became opaque. Gage showed no sign that he noticed, and continued staring through the glass.

"Mom, what's happening?" Sky whispered. She felt blindly for her mother's hand before remembering neither of them had any substance inside the memory.

"The house knows I don't want you to see this part of its memory, so it has shut itself off."

"What is Gage doing?"

A moment passed before Lily spoke again. "Gage has a gift for making others see what he wants them to see. And whatever he was making your grandfather see inside that house sent him after his wife and daughters with a meat cleaver."

The memory faded, and this time Sky knew she was back in her own time, in her own body. She shivered under the blanket next to her mother.

"The house has showed you everything that happened here, though, hasn't it?"

Lily nodded. "It needed to be heard. It doesn't show me as often now as it used to when we first moved here, so I think its wounds are fading."

"You talk about the house like it's a living thing."

"Gui's family was happy here; it was their home. Gage destroyed that in a matter of minutes, turned it into a husk bathed in their blood. That trauma inhabits the house now, but underneath it is the happiness the Rousseaus brought to it while they lived here. It's the reason I've never said anything to your father about this. If he knew what I saw, he'd insist we move somewhere else, and he would lose his only connection to his family. I'd never take that from him, so the house and I have learned to accept one another."

"But you still come out here a lot."

Her mother squeezed her hand. "We do whatever's necessary to get over the past." Lily's words were so close to what Gui had said about leading *a quiet life* that Sky's throat clogged with tears. He might not be her father by blood, but he loved her and her mother. Lily smiled. "And it helps having a happy family around you."

"So now that I know what it is you do, does that mean you'll be able to help me remember what happened to me the night I fell from the pier?"

Lily shook her head slowly. "If you can't remember it, I won't be able to see it, either."

They sat listening to the creak of the old swing for a minute or so.

"That kinda sucks," Sky said finally, and her mother nodded, her eyes looking down the hill toward the pier.

"It kinda does."

❖ 22 ❖

THE BLACKFINS GLIDED through the water, dipping below the surface and emerging to spurt jets of water from their blowholes moments later, like it was a game.

Sky watched them from the pier, her legs swinging over the edge. She'd avoided going home after school, not sure what to say to her dad now that she knew Severin was her biological father. If she even needed to say anything at all. Knowing hadn't changed the man who'd raised her.

With her mother working a late shift at the diner, Sky had headed down to the pier to figure out how she was going to shake loose the memory of what had happened on the night of her party.

And if Mom can see my memories, do I really want her to know what happened with Sean after the fight he had with Randy? That's just way TMI.

Sky leaned her head forward onto the horizontal bar of the guardrail.

"You look like you're about to jump in."

Sky jerked around at the sound of Jared's voice, and found him striding toward her along the boardwalk.

"Get out of my head!"

She hadn't meant to shout it, and after the silence-that-wasn't of Jared speaking to her, yet *not*, the noise startled them both. He joined her, his long legs swinging closer to the dark water than Sky's.

"Sorry."

"I didn't mean to yell. I'm just a little sick of creepy tricks like that." Sky gestured vaguely toward his legs. "Are you all right, after the other night, I mean?"

Out of the corner of her eye she saw him nod. Sky kept her eyes on the blackfins breaking through the dark water in front of her, there one moment and gone the next, hidden by the sky's reflection.

"Where do you fit into all this, Jared?"

He didn't insult her by pretending not to know what she meant. He didn't say anything at all. Instead, he took a roll of mints from his pocket, passing one to her before taking one himself. Sky held the hard candy in her hand for a moment before she let it drop into the churning water below.

"You could have just said you didn't want one."

She got to her feet, smoothing her skirt down where it had creased from sitting so long in the damp air.

"Have you somehow been sending me back to the circus? Is it your fault I keep landing back there?"

He was so long in answering, she didn't think he was going to.

"I'll see you around, I guess." She started to walk back along the pier.

"Sky, wait." She heard the sound of him scrambling to follow her but didn't turn around at first. "The first time, yes. I guided you while you were asleep back to the circus sixteen years ago. I *had* to. But it wasn't me after that, you went back by yourself. I just tagged along that time when you saw Madame Curio."

"It was you I saw that night outside my house!" Sky remembered all too clearly the outline reflected in the darkened TV screen, how she'd thought she was imagining things after her bizarre encounter at the circus. "You're working with Gage, aren't you?"

His expression darkened. "You think I want to? You think I have any say in it? He never lets me . . . GAH!"

Jared raked his hands back through his hair.

"I thought we were friends. I thought you liked my dad, that you were trying to help me figure out all this weirdness. But you weren't trying to help me. You've been pushing me further and further into it all along!"

Even if he was telling the truth, and he'd only started the process, he'd still had no right to turn her life upside down like that.

"Sky, I am your friend. I–"

She took a step away from him when he reached for her arm. "Jared, just stay the hell away from me!"

He looked stunned. Shoving his hands in his pockets, he marched past her with his shoulders hunched high against the cold breeze, and stopped.

"Believe it or not, I *was* trying to help you. As much as he'd let me, anyway."

Then he was gone.

Sky sank down against a wooden guard post, drawing her knees up to her chin. The wind would have been enough of an excuse for her tears, but she still refused to cry.

It wasn't just Jared. It wasn't that she knew her dad wasn't actually her father, and that she didn't know how to talk to him about it. It wasn't just the Swivellers. It wasn't what her mother had shown her or the creepiness of living in a house where her grandfather had murdered his entire family. It wasn't even that the man behind the murders seemed to keep appearing, becoming a part of her existence like a malignant growth. It was *everything*.

Sean had become the only one she felt sure of, and at the same time, the least sure. She knew her feelings for him were real. Even before this storm of craziness had swept her up, she had been drawn to him. But not like now, like some magnetic pull kept bringing her back to him.

And he felt it, too, she was sure of it. The way he held her hand, as though it was the most natural thing in the world. It was as though she was caught on an elastic line between Sean and the circus, and she had no idea what either of them wanted from her.

But she knew that wasn't fair.

Sean had never asked anything of her. He never kept things from her, never pushed her in one direction or another. Just thinking about Sean made her want to see him, to be near him.

"Well, you might," the old woman said from her left, and Sky jerked her head up to look at Madame Curio. She was impeccably dressed in a tweed suit with neat brown brogues on her feet, which was in itself as shocking as the sudden appearance of the old gypsy woman. "He anchors you here, and you him. Better to love the one you are tied to than feel him weighing you down like . . . well, like an anchor."

Sky smiled thinly. "How wonderfully cryptic."

One toe of a brown brogue jabbed Sky in the shin.

"Hey!"

"That remark sounded more like your friend with all the eyeliner. It's not time for self-pity now, child. There are things to be done before he arrives."

"Before *who* arrives?"

"Gage, of course. The boy was given a task, but allowed his feelings for you to get in the way. Now he comes to deal with matters himself, and wherever he goes, evil follows."

Sky drew her legs farther from the offending brogues before she answered. "What does Gage want?"

The old woman looked exasperated for a second, but then her features softened. "He wants an anchor, but he needs you to get it for him."

Anchor. That was what she had called Sean a few minutes earlier. *What would Gage want with Sean?*

"You will discover the rest soon enough. I must be going now."

"Going? Where?"

But that addled look had settled over Madame Curio's face again as she turned to look at the distant forms of the whales cutting the waves.

"He took my mind, you know. Made me see too much."

With brisk steps she walked to the end of the pier, and Sky watched in fascination as the old woman bent to retie her shoelace before climbing up onto the guardrail.

"Hey! Madame Curio, it's not safe!"

"If you want any more answers, child, you'll know where to find me."

Madame Curio lifted one foot from the guardrail, and fell backward.

"No!" Sky lunged forward to catch her, but the spot where Madame Curio had been was already empty, and Sky crashed into the guardrail. With a crack like a whip, it splintered under her hands, and Sky had a second to take in the circle of bubbles where the woman had hit the water before she plunged in after her. Cold swallowed her like a suit of needles. Darkness swallowed everything else.

Sky struggled frantically, kicking at the long skirt that wrapped around her legs. She couldn't see Madame Curio, couldn't see anything. Her lungs burned after only a few seconds, demanding that she return to the surface for air or be consumed by fire from within.

But the surface was too far away, the movement of the tide much stronger than it had looked from the pier. Another few seconds, and she could no longer feel the needles cutting into her hands. She could no longer feel her hands at all, and that was much worse.

Sean.

The thought had no focus. Still, it was enough to keep her fighting for the surface even as the feeling completely left her arms, then her legs. Thinking Sean's name was pulling at her, drawing her . . .

Sean.

The blackness was in her now, bleeding in through her mouth, her nose, her skin. She lost the thought, lost the thread that had been pulling her away. Now she could feel nothing, knew nothing, only darkness.

❧ 23 ❧

CHIMING, TINKLING ... ALMOST like laughter, but too metallic.

Sky struggled to open her eyes, but it was too much effort. Instead she lay with grass and sawdust sticking to her numb flesh. Only her throat burned where she must have retched up the salty water.

She felt nothing else, saw nothing else, only heard the bells. And then his voice.

"Ladies and gentlemen! Prepare yourselves to be shocked and amazed, as our next performer faces the feral Amazonian wolves!"

The band Sky had heard on her first visit to the Big Top started up a heart-thumping introduction, but above it Sky could still hear the gasps of the audience as they took in the spectacle Severin was laying before them.

"That's right, ladies and gentlemen! Our next performer is none other than the Wolfboy, whose talents and tricks will bedazzle and bewilder every last one of you—at only three years of age!"

Now Sky understood the gasps, and she forced her eyes to open. She was once again lying beneath the grandstand. Through the sloping slats above her she could see the twitching footwear of the crowd, and as she craned to see through the lowest section of the stands she could see the Wolfboy standing in the middle of the circus ring.

His skin looked pinched as he stared wide-eyed at the crowd gawping at him from every direction. He was barely old enough to be walking, yet the tot had been dressed in a garish ensemble of fur and tassels, with a hat fashioned to look like a wolf's head teetering atop his own.

Miss Schwarz's son. But where is she?

In the shadow of the wolf's eerie grin, the boy's eyes searched the crowd.

"Watch as Wolfboy entrances and beguiles the savage wolves!"

A faint cry escaped Sky's lips as three enormous gray wolves— the same wolves she had seen battering against the inside of their cage on her earlier visit—slunk into the arena. They hunched low, staying to the edges of the ring where the crowds were out of their sight. Only the boy, alone in the middle of the ring, was directly visible to them now, and they seemed curious about him. One by one they edged nearer, and Sky held her breath. The band played on somewhere beyond the stands, but all else was deathly silent. Until one of the wolves began to growl.

The tiny child stayed absolutely still at the center of the ring, as though he had been drilled for the situation.

Which he has, of course, Sky told herself, trying to find some way of feeling better because of that. But the terror in the little boy's eyes was unmistakable, and Sky tried to push herself to her feet. She needed to help him, get him out of there somehow. But almost drowning had robbed her muscles of their strength, the cold still bone deep inside her. Only her fingers burned where feeling had begun to return to them, hot prickles in her flesh.

Her arm slid out from under her when she tried to hoist herself into a sitting position, and she hit the dirt, choking on a cloud of sawdust.

"See the hunters as they stalk their prey, their world contained within the transparent walls of the ring! Now watch as the hunters' world is turned on its head!"

Sky could only see through a tiny gap under the bleachers, but a second later, the wolves inside the arena had all rolled over and were yelping and kicking their legs into the air as though they expected to be dragged up into it at any moment.

"But when their prize is so near at hand, nothing can hold them at bay for long!"

At Severin's announcement, the wolves righted themselves and turned as a unit to face the tiny figure in the center of the circle.

"No no no no . . ."

Her throat burning, Sky could only chant the word over and over again in a whisper, her limbs too dull and heavy to allow her to move.

Why is Severin doing this?

Her sense of betrayal was sudden and sharp. Could this man really be her father?

The wolves growled as they stalked closer to the boy. But something was peculiar. For all that the boy looked frightened, he also appeared to be concentrating deeply, his brow creased with the effort.

The wolves lunged as one, and Sky's heart all but exploded. But instead of tearing into the boy, they all simply froze.

What the hell is going on?

Severin stepped into the arena now, parading around the edge as the crowd cheered. The boy stood statue-still, arms by his sides and staring straight ahead, all three wolves posed mid-lunge with their teeth bared and ready for tearing.

"Put your hands together, ladies and gentleman, for the incredible Wolfboy!"

The crowd cheered even more loudly, but Sky still heard one voice yelling above the others.

"They're not even real! I bet you, they're not real! Look!"

Sky couldn't see the man, but she saw the half-eaten candy apple he threw, sending it sailing straight at one of the wolves. The tiny boy looked up as it landed near him, and the spell was broken.

Sky saw fear becoming absolute horror in his eyes, and the wolves lunged forward like their attack had never been interrupted. A hundred voices in the crowd screamed, and then the child was gone, clutched to Severin's chest under the bleachers next to Sky.

Inside the ring, a net fell onto the wolves, trapping them.

There's no way he could have reached the boy so quickly, especially not without being mauled by the wolves.

Yet the ringmaster stood over her, breathing hard, and looking slightly more rumpled than she had seen him on previous occasions. The child whimpered as Severin held him close.

"I sensed you were nearby," Severin said, kneeling in the sawdust. "I've been carrying a letter for you, hoping you'd come back. Gage saw you the last time you were here, sweetness. He doesn't know who you are, but he's looking for you. You need to get out of here, as far away as you can."

Sky glared at him, not believing he could be concerned with something like that after he'd just let the boy almost get killed.

"There's no point in giving me those eyes, *chère*. Little Jimmy here ain't mine to control." Sky remembered seeing the boy racing past her and Jared when they'd first visited the circus together, his red-haired mother—Miss Schwarz, she now realized—running after him.

How could she allow him to be used like this? She didn't get the chance to speculate further, as Severin had taken a rather rumpled envelope from the pocket of his red coat and was waving it at her.

"Here, take this."

She could barely feel the crackle of the paper with her frozen fingers.

"You do look a mite ill, *chère*. Perhaps you should be heading back to wherever you call home, yes?"

Sky coughed, and the effort physically hurt. "Not where, *when*."

The audience continued to holler and wail in confusion at what they had seen, at what they *couldn't* have seen.

Above her head, wood splintered with an ugly cracking noise. A groan of metal followed seconds later, and the crowd above her head began to panic anew.

But then silence descended, sudden and unnatural. Severin leaned down toward Sky so he could see through the same gap where she saw Gage standing at the center of the ring.

The wolves were gone, and Gage stood with one finger raised, a teacher silencing a classroom of wayward children. His face was painted white, black circling his eyes and lips underneath the brim of his bowler hat. The consummate mime, his audience was captivated.

It was horrific to watch, to *feel* his power creeping out of him, wrapping around the people he held enthralled.

Sky couldn't see the crowd from where she lay, but she sensed the tension in them. Whatever had made the wolves freeze mid-lunge a few moments earlier now held them still, paralyzed in the middle of their panic as though they were being electrocuted.

"Dammit!" Severin hissed. "He knows he can't control them all without the skull."

The amber skull.

As though to confirm Sky's suspicion, Severin held it out for a second, the light slanting between the bleachers catching it, making the sinister depths of its empty eye sockets glow orange.

Severin shoved it into the pocket of his red ringmaster's coat.

"You stole it?"

Severin nodded, but his gaze was still locked on Gage. "Not that it was really stealing, since the skull was mine to begin with. But I've given them a chance to get away, at least," he said. "Gage won't be able to hold them under his spell for long without doing permanent damage to their minds. He might not be able to hold such a large crowd for long, anyway."

The bleachers above them groaned, and the sound of something snapping farther along the row bore down on them. Sky fought to move her jellied limbs, but she was still half paralyzed with cold. Severin's eyes locked on hers, and she could see he understood.

"I'll be seeing you soon, *chère*. Get you gone, now. I'd better get this one out of here."

With that, Severin disappeared just as a board gave out above where he had been standing with the boy in his arms.

"Wait! The boy—you have to save him from the fire." But she was calling out to thin air. Sky closed her eyes, waiting for the stands over her head to collapse. Snapping, groaning, so near.

Flashing light, sparks in her brain.

A strange sound, but one that was comforting all the same.

Someone singing. That's what it is.

Sean.

She focused on that thought, let it draw her toward that splinter of light which beckoned from behind her eyelids.

That's it! She could feel it working, pulling her out of one moment and into another. She could see Sean like a beacon, so easy for her to reach out for; an anchor in a swirling abyss.

Her body grew lighter, limbs filled with nothing but air and sparks, and she hurled herself like a lightning bolt along the pathway.

❦ 24 ❦

SKY LOOKED DOWN and discovered that she was bundled up in what appeared to be Sean's soccer jersey, jeans, cardigan, duffle coat, hat, scarf, and gloves. When she rolled her head to the side, she saw Sean was driving in only a pair of shorts and a T-shirt, no shoes. He had apparently laced his sneakers onto her feet over her own soggy socks.

In the darkness outside Sean's Jeep, Sky could see the craggy rise of the Lychgate Mountains crowding up to meet them in the narrow beams of the headlights. The rocks sparkled, the first ice of the season clinging to the already treacherous mountain road.

"Thank God you're awake. I think you're suffering from hypothermia, so we're on our way to the hospital." Sean's eyes darted to meet hers before returning to the road, but his pinched look of panic eased slightly as Sky met his gaze.

"Are you sure we should be going to the hospital? I mean, how are we going to explain this—"

"I'm taking you to the hospital. I lost you once because I didn't act fast enough. I won't do that again."

"Thanks." Sky lifted one hand to the wet tangle of Sean's hair that was dripping down onto his T-shirt. "I think you're the one who'll need treatment for hypothermia, though."

He gave her a small smile. "I'm not going to lie, I'm bloody cold." When she moved to take off his borrowed coat he almost skidded off the road. "Will you leave the coat on, for Christ's sake?"

Sky laughed, even though it hurt her throat. Still, she did as he'd asked.

"What are we going to tell them at the hospital?"

He glanced at her. "I don't know. How *did* you end up soaking wet in the guys' locker room?"

Then Sky remembered Madame Curio. "Oh God, Sean! Madame Curio jumped off the pier—she must be dead."

Sean pulled the car to the side of the road. "I'd better call Aunt Holly."

Gravel popped and crunched beneath the tires as they eased onto the shoulder. Sean dipped his hand into the pocket of the duffle coat she was wearing and fished out his cell. The display made strange shadows over his face as he held the phone to his ear, but then he frowned as he looked at it.

"No signal. I'll have to call her when we get to the—"

Sky couldn't immediately tell why he had stopped short, but saw that his eyes were fixed on the rearview mirror. Without looking away, Sean killed the headlights and turned off the engine.

"What is it?"

Sean's expression became inscrutable as the light on his cell display went out. "There's a red car following us up the hill.

Whoever's in it just turned their headlights off."

Sky wasn't sure what this meant, but Sean's tone made it clear he thought it was bad.

"Do you think they've broken down or something?"

His head turned toward her, but she still couldn't see his face in the darkness. "I think whoever's following us doesn't want us to see them coming."

"What do we do?"

"Nothing much we can do, really. Except hope their car's not four-wheel drive, like this one."

He turned the ignition again and flipped on his headlights before pulling back onto the road.

"Someone taped an anonymous note to my window Saturday night. It said they know what I am—a Pathfinder—and that if I didn't stay away from him—whoever *him* is—I'd have to deal with the consequences."

Even as she spoke, Sky watched the mirror in the side door for any sign of a vehicle closing in on them. It was too dark to see far behind them, especially with no headlights to give the other vehicle away.

"What does *Pathfinder* mean?" Sean's tone was carefully neutral.

"That's what Severin called himself. He says we can travel the pathways of different realities, like tracing lines on a map."

"We?"

"Maybe Severin's the one the note-writer wants me to stay away from."

"Sixteen years in the past?"

"I guess so," she said.

He looked at her for a second before he burst out laughing. And kept laughing. "I think my brain just melted."

"Hey! We're being chased by some weirdo who writes threatening notes, remember?"

"Maybe. I mean, we don't know it's the same person. Do you still have it?"

"I don't have that one, but I *do* have one Severin gave me."

She had to undo the button fly on Sean's borrowed jeans to get to her own jeans pocket underneath, and her fingers were stiff and unhelpful. Finally, she tugged the crinkled paper free of its sheath and squinted to read it.

"Here, use the torch on my phone."

Sky took Sean's cell phone, and studied the letter. It wasn't an explanation of how she'd become a Pathfinder, nor did it shed any light on the events sixteen years ago, which had led *someone* to chase her off Blackfin Pier. Still, she grinned.

"What? What is it, Sky?"

She held up the drawing, the series of intersecting lines and almost endless branches invisible to Sean in the dark. It was a map of sorts—the pathways laid out on paper, with a mark showing Sky exactly what Severin wanted her to see: where and when to find him. "It's an invitation."

The car lurched sharply, throwing Sky against the inside of the door.

"Shit! They've caught up."

"What do we do?"

"Try my cell again. Call the police if you can. *Shit!*"

There was a screech of tires as the vehicle chasing them slid on the icy road trying to build enough speed to ram them again. Sean's eyes narrowed.

"Brace yourself, Sky. I'm going to slam on the brakes."

Sky checked her seat belt and grabbed hold of the armrest just as Sean hit the brakes. The jolt threw Sky forward, the seat belt digging painfully into her shoulder. The crash sounded like a bomb going off, and was followed by a hiss of steam from the car behind them. It chugged off onto the hard shoulder.

"Are you okay?"

"Yeah. What about your car—?"

"The car's fine. I have a tow hitch on the back, so the other car is probably pretty mangled right now." He laughed, and Sky whacked him on the arm.

"This isn't funny, Sean! Someone just tried to kill us."

"Somehow I don't really think Miss Schwarz wanted us dead. The note didn't say anything about killing you, did it? And that's assuming it was even from her."

"Miss Schwarz?"

Sean nodded and restarted the car. To Sky's surprise it started up right away, and then they were driving through the mountain pass again as though nothing had happened.

"I recognized her car."

"Do you think she might be hurt?"

Sean shook his head. "The impact sounded a lot worse than it actually was. I could see her yelling at us as we pulled off. She looked more pissed than hurt."

"But why would she be following us?" Sean didn't know about Miss Schwarz's son. Sky quickly filled him in on what she knew. "But why would she have written the note?" Sky wondered aloud. "I had nothing to do with what happened to her little boy. And who is she warning me to stay away from?"

Sean shook his head. "I guess that's something we'll have to ask her. But first, I'm getting you to the hospital. You still don't look the right color."

"But I feel—"

Sky stiffened at a flash of light up ahead, thinking she was about to fade again. But these lights were blue, and racing past them up into the Lychgate Mountains.

Patrol cars.

"I wonder if they've been called out because of the crash," Sean said.

"Maybe somebody found Madame Curio." Either way, Sky hoped they'd find her soon, before her body got swept away on the tide.

❧ 25 ❧

ONE DIAGNOSIS OF mild hypothermia later, Sky lay in the hospital bed waiting for her parents to arrive. Sean's voice drifted in from the hallway where he was calling his aunt—partly to let her know what had happened with the accident and Madame Curio, and partly to find out which one the patrol cars were responding to.

They had agreed to fudge the truth a little about how Sky had come to be shivering with cold, her own clothes still soggy beneath the layers Sean had piled over them. As far as the hospital staff were aware, Sky had tried to save Madame Curio but ended up having to wade back to the beach, where Sean had spotted her as he drove home from soccer practice. They'd raised a few eyebrows when they saw Sky's medical records, the marker strike through the red DECEASED stamp showing she had suffered a similar misadventure only a few months earlier.

Teen suicide, their expressions said as they wrote her off. It also explained why they didn't seem concerned about finding out what had become of Madame Curio's body.

Sean's expression was grim as he reentered.

"Sky, I'm afraid your parents won't be here for a while yet."

A fist grabbed her heart and squeezed it painfully. "Has something happened to them?"

"Oh, no! They're *fine*, Sky. It's not them, it's the Swiveller brothers."

Her relief at knowing her parents were fine made her brain sluggish. "What about them?"

Sean took the seat next to the bed. "They were in an accident. Felix's car went over the Point, with all four brothers inside. Looks like the ice must have caused the car to skid . . ."

He didn't need to finish. Sky could imagine it all too well, sailing over the edge of that sheer cliff face and plummeting into the dark abyss below. She shuddered.

"Are they . . . ?" Sean nodded, and Sky had to focus on her fingernails for a little while. "Oh God, that's awful." When she looked up at Sean again, he was smiling at her. "What?"

"I'm just amazed you can feel bad for them after what they did to you."

Sky considered. *Did* she feel bad for them? Or was it just the shocking way they'd died?

"It's got to be terrible for their parents. No matter what they did, Mr. and Mrs. Swiveller didn't deserve to lose all their kids. And I've known them my whole life—they're like Silas up on the school roof, or the blackfins down at the pier: always there, a part of the town." *But not anymore.* "But that doesn't explain why my parents aren't here."

Sean fidgeted uncomfortably. "Aunt Holly told me that a witness saw a man get out of the Swivellers' car just before it drove over the cliff, and that the car didn't even brake before it reached the edge. They're asking your dad some questions because he knows about car stuff, and because of what happened to you."

Sky went cold. "You think my dad did it? Like, cut their brakes or something? How could you even *think* that?"

Sean looked pained. "I don't know, Sky. Maybe I'm wrong, but all I know is that *I* thought about killing those freaks after what they did to you, so I wouldn't blame your dad for thinking the same."

"My dad would never do something like that!" Sky knew it, believed it without question. He was the man she loved most in the world, the one who would take care of his *coco* no matter what. He wasn't some monster who murdered people in cold blood.

"Both your parents are at Oakridge Station right now," Sean said. "My aunt's asked me to stay with you, and take you home when they discharge you."

Sky didn't even hear the last part. "Jared!" Sean looked at her, confused. "Jared works with my dad at the garage. He'd probably know as much about cutting someone's brakes as my dad would!"

Sean reached for her hand. "But why would Jared want to kill the Swivellers?"

Sky sank back into the stiff hospital bed. "Why does Jared do anything?" Despite her words, she knew Sean had a point. Her dad had a motive to kill the Swivellers. What could Jared's motive be?

"Cam and Bo are on their way here, too. They're worried about you." Sean stroked the hair from her face with his free hand. Sky felt her eyelids getting heavier, the weight of the cold water and everything that had happened forcing them to close. "But you should get some sleep. I'll stay here and fill them in when they arrive."

She only had the energy to nod before she was swallowed by dreamless darkness.

❧❧❧

EVEN WHEN SHE whispered, Cam Vega's voice could cut glass.

"You promised me you'd be nice to her, and that means making sure she doesn't die again, idiot!"

Cam almost never got angry, and in truth, it was more amusing than intimidating, like an irate squirrel.

"I'm trying to—" Sean's reply was cut short as Bo chimed in, her voice dry as sawdust.

"It doesn't seem like you're making her terribly happy if she keeps throwing herself off the pier."

"She wasn't trying to kill herself, though."

At least one of her friends believed that. Sky sat up in bed to give them a piece of her mind, but the spinning in her head forced her to lie back down.

"So what the hell *is* going on with her?"

Sean didn't answer, and Sky couldn't blame him. She hadn't explained any of this to her friends, and now the mess had grown so gigantic she didn't know where to begin.

"I can hear you, you know."

At the sound of her voice, they all filtered in through the swing-door, looking sheepish. Well, except Bo, who only looked peeved that she couldn't light the roll-up hanging from her fingers.

"So, what's up?" Bo asked, taking the uncomfortable visitor chair and throwing her feet onto the mattress next to Sky. Cam perched at the foot of the hospital bed, and Sean settled back to lean against the wheeled medical cart in the corner. It suddenly seemed a long way from her.

In the time it took her to blink at the split-second flash of light, Sky was leaning against the cabinet next to him. Everyone, including Bo, jumped.

"So . . . I guess I have some explaining to do."

⚜

EVERYONE LISTENED IN silence as Sky explained all that had been happening to her over the last few weeks: the first visit to the circus, which Jared had engineered, the shifts that had shown her alternate versions of the present and the past, everything that had led her to the circus, to Gage, and to Severin—the ringmaster who claimed she was like him.

A Pathfinder.

"So, you really *didn't* mean to just disappear for three months?" Bo squinted at her uncertainly.

Sky shook her head. "Of course not."

"And you're saying a Pathfinder is someone who's been displaced from their own reality-timeline-thing at the point where they were meant to die, and after that they can just travel to alternate dimensions and different times and shit?"

"Pretty much," Sky said, "except I think we can always *see* the alternate stuff, even before we're able to travel there. It's just that after we're . . . *displaced* . . . then we can just move through the barriers that normally keep everything separate and go wherever, whenever we want."

"As long as it's within your own life, though, right?" Cam chirped, then looked bashful when everyone turned to stare at her. "I mean, there are so many points in history you could have traveled to, so many places you could have gone, but you've pretty much stayed in Blackfin. You've never traveled to any place or time where you didn't already exist."

It was like a curtain had been lifted. "So *that's* the connection! That's why I'm zipping around like I'm on some giant bungee cord—because I basically *am*. It's like I'm tethered to my *true* pathway, and even though I can hop over to other realities or even go back into the past, I'm always connected to my own present."

"But what's the cord tied to?" Sean asked. "And who's this Gage guy who seems to be a feature of your trips to the past *and* now?"

Sky considered. "I can answer the first one. Severin told me that a Pathfinder always has an anchor, and that's something that's tied to the decision I made, which led me to where I should have died."

"What's your anchor, then? The pier?"

"It's you, asshat." Bo dropped her feet from the bed and stood up. "Man, this is going to get awkward when you two break up. I need to go and have a smoke so I can process." She left without waiting for any response. Cam looked from Bo's retreating figure to Sean and Sky and back again.

"We won't be long!"

The door swung shut with a clatter after she ran through it. Sky nudged Sean with her shoulder.

"Are you freaking out?"

He dipped his head to one side. "I don't like not knowing what's going on with this Gage guy, but I wouldn't say I'm freaking out, no."

Sky laughed. "I meant about the whole anchor thing."

He grinned back at her. "I know you did. And no, I'm not. But how does it work? If you needed me, could I find you, or does it just work one way?"

Sky considered. "So far, whenever I've needed to get out or find my way back home, I've just thought about you and I kind of get pulled to wherever you are. Like no matter where I've traveled in time or whatever, I can find my way back by looking for you. Even now, I know I could go tearing off into the pathways if I tried, but while you're here next to me, you keep me grounded." She chewed her lip, feeling Sean's eyes on her.

"I like the idea that wherever—whenever—you go, you can always find your way back here, to me. Now I don't feel so helpless, like you're just going to disappear from my life again."

Sky studied her nails. "Sean, there's something else. My mom can relive people's memories. She showed me what happened at my house before my dad inherited it. I didn't see all of it, but I know that what happened was pretty grisly. But she can't see what happened to me on the night I fell from the pier—the first time, I mean—because I can't remember it myself. I don't remember anything after I ran from the school down onto the promenade."

Sean waited in silence for her to make her point.

"I think I need to go back to that night, to see exactly what happened to me. If it was Gage chasing me, I need to know why. Until I know what he wants from me, I feel like I can't protect myself."

"What do you need me to do?"

"Could you take me home, and stay with me until I . . . well, stay there until I get back?"

He leaned over and kissed her, just as she needed him to. "Of course I will."

❧ 26 ❧

SILAS SPUN DIZZYINGLY fast above Sky as she watched him from next to Sean's Jeep. Checking the time on the rusted hands of the clock, she guessed there were a few minutes until Sean and Randy would come barging through the side door of the gymnasium and start fighting in the lot.

The side door swung open, exhaling Bo into the balmy night air. Sky had forgotten that the two boys had not been the first to leave the gymnasium that night. Bo walked to the corner of the building, already shielding the flame of her Zippo with one hand as she lit her roll-up.

Bo paced briskly, never straying out of sight of the door, plumes of smoke wafting after her. She finished her cigarette, rolled and lit another.

"Bo!"

The exaggerated whisper would have been enough to reveal Cam's identity even without her springing through the door like a jack-in-the-box. Bo stopped pacing.

"Shouldn't you be inside?"

"Can I have a smoke?"

Sky frowned. The only time both Cam and Bo had left her at

the party, Cam had said she was going to the bathroom. And Cam didn't smoke. At least, she hadn't thought so.

"Here." Bo handed over the roll-up she'd just lit. Cam drew in a deep breath like she'd been gasping for it.

"Thanks. Do you think—"

At that moment the door flew open, the metal handle ringing as it struck the crumbling outer wall, knocking some small chunks to the pavement. Cam, quick as a cat, dropped her cigarette and disappeared around the corner of the school. Bo ground the cigarette out with her heel before she vanished around the same corner as Cam.

Sean and Randy appeared, shoving at each other until they reached the edge of the lot, close to where Sky crouched next to Sean's Jeep.

"Why do you have to stick your ugly nose into business that's not yours, Vega?"

Randy grabbed a handful of Sean's cardigan and tried to lever him to the ground, but Sean, tugging himself free, elbowed Randy in the windpipe.

"Because you were being a dick"—Sean said, sidestepping as Randy tried to kick him—"and Sky didn't look like she wanted you mauling her." He threw his fist at Randy's face, only connecting with his ear as Randy ducked.

"But it's none of your business!" Randy actually spat, and Sean looked down at where the spittle glistened in a streak against his sneaker. Randy used the moment to punch the side of Sean's head, and Sean stumbled backward. "Only *I'm* allowed to have her. *He* said so."

"*He?* What are you talking—"

Sky saw herself appear behind the two boys, her hair shining golden even in the silvery light. Her long dress swirled around her ankles like little fish caught in a current. Even the scuffed boots she'd worn to spite her mother were oddly chic.

Her other self was so composed, her every movement fluid and graceful. It reminded her of watching Severin perform in the Big Top.

Had she not been trying to remain hidden, she might have laughed. It wasn't the way her past self looked, exactly—nothing as simple as a pretty girl in a swishy dress—or even the way her movements seemed to draw in the moonlight rather than reflect it. Everything about this girl held Sky spellbound, as though she had no choice but to watch her, to want to remain in her orbit forever.

It was what made people want to be close to her. And similar to her drawing the fish to her father's net with a mere flicker of her fingers in the water, this magnetism wasn't natural.

Sky realized it was true, too, of Randy's reaction to her at the party. He had wanted something from her, and she was beginning to see how that *coveting* might become twisted inside the warped brain of a Swiveller when it was denied.

Sky watched Randy run off, not onto Main Street and toward his home as she had supposed, but onto the bluff overlooking the promenade.

Then the most mortifying moment of her life replayed in front of her. With the oddest pang of jealousy, Sky watched her former self move in to kiss Sean, saw him pull away gently. Then she watched herself overreact like an idiot.

Holding her hand to her mouth, the other Sky rose smoothly to her feet and fled, her skirts trailing behind her.

"Sky, wait! I–"

"Leave me alone!"

Sean stared in silence for a moment, then leaned back onto the grass which edged the parking lot, raking his hands back through his hair. He groaned, and Sky fought the urge to go and hug him. But she couldn't do that, knew that if she did anything in this version of her past that differed from the one she had lived, it would diverge into another reality, and she wouldn't see what had really happened to her on the pier.

Sky watched her other self disappear into the night, and turned to find Sean walking over to where she hid.

Panicking, she dropped soundlessly to the ground and rolled underneath Sean's Jeep, her heart thudding so loudly she was sure he'd feel it through the metal body of the car between them. The sound of his keys jangling as he brought them out presented a new problem: had Sean followed her down to the pier in his car? If so, she was about to have an unfortunate encounter with the underside of it.

"Oh, hey, Bo. What are you doing out here?"

"Teaching your sister how to blow smoke rings, of course."

Sean made a sound that wasn't quite a laugh.

"Look, I did something really dumb and upset Sky. I'm going to go and try to sort it out with her. . . ."

"You mean you finally made a move on her?"

Sky could almost hear the warring thoughts in Sean's head: should he say yes and protect Sky from any embarrassment, or tell the truth? In the end, he did neither.

"I got into a fight with Randy and was a bit of a dick to her about it."

"Ah."

"So, yeah. I'd, uh, better be going."

If Sky waited around to eavesdrop on the rest of the conversation, she would probably miss whatever happened to her at the pier, and would have wasted this trip back into the past. Maybe there was no limit to how many times she could travel back to a particular moment, but right now, she didn't want to risk finding out.

As quietly as possible, Sky slid out on the opposite side of the car from where Sean stood talking with Bo. If she stayed low and kept to the shadows behind the line of cars in the lot, there would only be a narrow gap where she would have to run within their line of sight. And even if they happened to see her, they would only see her silhouette at this distance—the silhouette of a girl wearing jeans and a baggy sweater, not the flowing skirts she'd worn to the party.

Sky reached the point where she would have to cross the open space to the school gates, and spared a glance over at Sean's car. From where she crouched she could no longer hear Sean and Bo talking, but his car engine hadn't started, either.

Maybe he went back inside the school?

It didn't matter. Sky ran for the gates, cleared them in a matter of seconds, and was on the path down to the promenade when she saw them.

Randy had taken the sandy footpath that ran parallel to the seafront, and had acquired an additional three Swivellers from somewhere.

Where had the other three been during the party? She only remembered seeing Randy there, but it was possible the others had also been at the school. But what were they doing now, looking down at the pier at night?

This is the last time you'll see them like this, she thought. Though it had happened so recently she hadn't quite processed what it would mean for life in Blackfin, four kids from her school were now dead. They were less than five bus-lengths away from her now, but when she returned to her own time, all four of them would be dead. No matter what the Swivellers had done to her, Sky couldn't feel good about that.

She needed to move. Standing still on the pathway behind them, she knew one of them would be bound to spot her if she didn't get out of there. But unless she went back to school and took cover in the parking lot, the only other place she could hide was next to the promenade wall.

The path leading down to the promenade was cut into the green, so that once a person was on the concrete path edging the seafront, they had a grass verge behind them to buffer the worst of the cold wind blowing in from the ocean. But to get to the promenade, Sky either had to run straight past the Swivellers or jump ten feet from the verge down onto the concrete path.

Her choice wasn't really a choice at all.

Sky glanced once more at the Swivellers before making her dash for the verge. They all stood as still as they had been before, none of them speaking, simply staring at something down on the wooden pier. Though Sky squinted in the dim light cast by the moon and a few grimy electric lanterns along the path, she couldn't see what had captivated them. There was no movement on the pier. Either her earlier self hadn't yet reached it, or she was already drowning in the water.

Unless something else happened to me in between, she realized. The witnesses who had said it was only a few minutes between when she had fled the party and when Sean had set out after her could have been mistaken. Twenty minutes could easily seem like five in hindsight.

And had Sean even gone directly to the pier?

She paused at the verge, looking down at the concrete below, glad she was wearing jeans to protect her knees if she did go sprawling. Sky braced herself and dropped.

She hadn't seen it in the shadows, but she was grateful for the wedge of windblown sand that cushioned her impact as she landed neatly on her feet with barely a sound.

Shaking sand from one of her boots, she looked over toward the pier.

Now she saw what the Swivellers were looking at.

27

A MAN STOOD watching at the foot of the cut leading down onto the promenade. He was directly in the Swivellers' line of sight, but invisible from where Sky had been, so she had no idea why they were staring at him at first.

She pressed herself back against the verge, thankful the position of the moon allowed her at least a narrow strip of shadow to hide in. Holding her breath, she watched from her hiding spot.

What the hell is he doing?

All she could see of the man's face was a sliver of jaw and ear, and this was in the shadow of a bowler hat.

Fear iced a path along her spine. Almost as though he had sensed her presence, Gage turned his head to the side and cocked it, listening. It was definitely him.

He wore none of the face paint that had given him the skeletal appearance of a mime, but he was no less frightening. His skin sagged around the hollows of his cheeks; his eyes were sunken in his head until all she could see of them was the fierce pinpoint of light spearing outward. Sixteen years may have passed since Sky had seen Gage at the circus, but there was nothing faded, nothing less severe about the man.

Gage held up one bony, pale hand and pointed out toward the end of the pier, where the crashing waves and wind seemed to inhale the silence.

Sky saw herself, her earlier self. She was standing at the farthest point, arms hugging her body against the cold. Sky remembered it now, remembered feeling stupid to be out sulking in the wind on her birthday.

Gage's hand shook with effort, and his teeth showed in a grimace of rage. Shoving his hand in his pocket, he turned, seemingly about to head back onto the green. But then he noticed the Swivellers, still standing in a tidy row, their black eyes fixed on Gage's figure like they were under a spell.

Under his spell, wasn't that how Severin had described it?

So why was Sky immune to his mind control? Because that was surely what he had been trying to do, pointing a shaking finger at her as she stood oblivious at the end of the pier.

He can't reach me without the skull.

The amber skull, which he didn't have now because Severin had stolen it from him sixteen years earlier.

The Swivellers walked toward Gage, who stood waiting for them with both arms outstretched like he was greeting long-lost friends.

Then it struck Sky: the Swivellers. If what Severin had told her of Gage's ability was true, and he was at this very moment using it on the Swivellers, then it must have driven them mad.

That was why they dug up my grave and kept the corpse. Why they tried to bury me alive.

She wasn't denying that the Swiveller brothers had all been a little creepy before the night of her party, but they had certainly taken a pretty sharp descent into psychopathy after that. Gage's influence had to be the reason.

Would that be reason enough to kill them? she wondered. *Gage could have used his mind tricks to make Felix drive over the cliff.*

The idea curdled in her brain. If Gage was getting rid of the evidence of what he'd done, surely she would be next. Except that it all seemed to be about activating her power, not killing her. Could that have been another reason for Gage to kill the Swivellers? Because they'd tried to bury her again?

What does Gage want with me?

Too many questions, and they almost distracted her from seeing the Swivellers advance. As they reached Gage, each dropped down onto all fours next to him, looking at where her other self stood staring down into the water at the end of the pier.

Were they seriously *growling?*

Stranger still, Gage reached down to pat the top of Jordy's head before pointing silently to the pier. All four boys leaped to their feet and ran for the boardwalk. Even above the sound of the wind and the waves lashing the shore, Sky heard their gleeful whoops.

Sky's other self must have heard the noise, too. She walked toward them, unconcerned. Of course, back then Sky had had no reason to fear the Swivellers, and had probably thought Randy and his brothers were simply goofing around on the promenade.

That was about to change.

"Randy, what are you—aah!"

Sky watched in horrified fascination as Randy body-slammed her former self to the wooden boards. She could tell the other Sky was winded from the way she lay, her mouth open and gasping for air, trying to bring her arms up to push Randy off. But Randy wasn't interested in withdrawing to let Sky catch her breath.

He grabbed a handful of her hair in his hand and lifted her head up off the boards, only to slam it back down with a sickening *thud*. The other Sky yelped and tried to curl in on herself, to roll out from under the boy's weight, but he had her pinned between his legs. His brothers edged nearer, scavengers waiting for the killing blow to land.

Gage was still some distance away at the foot of the pier, but Sky could tell even from where she hid that he was enjoying the scene before him. That horrid, twisted grin tugged at the sagging flesh of his face.

Felix reached the prone Sky's foot and pulled at the boot with his teeth. Sensing the interference, Randy snarled at his brother. The other Sky whimpered at the sound, but that only made Randy turn his attention back to her.

I remember that sound.

Gage strode forward, sweeping his arm to the side in a gesture that somehow carried the Swivellers away from her other self and to heel. Sky watched herself scrabble backward, obviously disoriented from the knock to her head. She backed up right against the guardrail, and stopped.

With a mocking finger-wave, Gage called his wolfboys on, and they leaped at her. They snarled and snapped, surging forward until the other Sky was forced to clamber up onto the rail. One step, two.

She had reached the point of no return, and gravity did the rest. But just as Sky expected to see her plummet down into the dark water, there was a blast of light.

By the time her eyes adjusted to the darkness again, she heard a splash that told her a body very much like her own had hit the water below.

That flash must have been the point at which I stole another Sky's life for three months.

Even though there was no way Sky could have known that at the time, and there was nothing she could have done to alter it, the guilt of having someone else—even though that someone else was still *her* in some sense—suffer the end which should have been Sky's just wasn't something she could deal with.

Sky shrank against the grass behind her, her tears turning icy as the wind blasted them from her cheeks. All had gone quiet on the pier, and she knew Gage and the Swivellers would be heading back in a matter of moments. Sean hadn't yet arrived, but she knew that it couldn't be long before he did. Before he dragged what he thought was *her* from the cold water and tried to save her.

I should never have come back here.

The wind stopped buffeting her, and she knew what that meant. Low growls came from the Swivellers, too close for them to miss her much longer, but still she couldn't move.

Then footsteps, racing across the grass above and behind her.

The Swivellers fell silent, and she opened her eyes just in time to see the last of them skulking off along the promenade. Sean hadn't noticed them, though—his eyes were fixed on the pier.

No, not the pier.

He had already seen the white speck floating in the water just off the beach and was vaulting over the promenade railing and down onto the beach below.

Sean!

Whatever trigger connected her to her anchor was pulled in that instant. Sky faded out, disappearing from a past that she never ever wanted to revisit again.

Lightning flashed behind her eyelids, and for the first time she truly, clearly saw the pathways stretching out—around, inside, *through* her. More than that, she saw that beacon, shining golden at a point in her own pathway, running strongest through her. She followed it, and the weight of reentering her own pathway was like the emptiness being refilled, and it was him.

Sean held her so tight against him that Sky couldn't breathe, didn't want to breathe ever again if it meant him letting go. She felt his lips, hot against her skin, and met them with her own, pushing him back onto her bed. The bed springs should have creaked in the empty house, but the Blood House swallowed the sound. Nothing else existed beyond the room they were in. Not death or mind control or the dark water gnashing its teeth against the struts of Blackfin Pier.

"Did you see what happened?"

Sky nodded, but couldn't talk about that. Couldn't let herself think about what she had seen, what had been done to throw her life into such chaos.

She needed to be lost, and for Sean to anchor her in that moment.

Sky leaned back, tugged the oversized sweater over her head. Sean stared up at her, eyes wide as they traced her skin. Still, he held back. She knew what he would ask and gave him the only answer she could.

"I need you, Sean."

There were no more questions, only his arms around her, his heat against her skin, and the perfection of being lost and found in a heartbeat.

❧ 28 ❧

A DOOR SLAMMED somewhere in the house, and a moment later Sky heard her father's voice booming from the downstairs hallway.

"Coco?"

She froze in her bed as his footsteps began climbing the stairs, and Sean's arm tightened around her waist. He'd heard it, too.

"The window!" she whispered, and Sean's eyes darted to it, but then he shook his head. He slid out of her bed and dressed hurriedly.

"I'll go and speak with your dad. I don't want to go sneaking around behind his back."

"Are you crazy?"

Sean smiled at her. "Maybe a little."

"Please, Sean! I couldn't bear it if they told me not to see you anymore."

The heavy footsteps continued their approach. They didn't hurry, so Sky said a silent prayer of thanks to the Blood House for muting their conversation. Still, Sean hesitated, one sneaker still unlaced.

Stubborn boy!

Sky dived for her bathrobe on the back of her bedroom door just as Gui's footfalls stopped on the other side of it.

Please! she mouthed silently, and Sean moved reluctantly toward the french windows. They opened before he'd even reached them, allowing him a silent exit onto the balcony. He rolled his eyes, climbed over the railing, and disappeared.

Gui knocked on the door.

"Coco?"

Sky fastened the tie tightly around her waist and opened the door, wearing what she hoped was a breezy smile. "Dad! You're home!"

He narrowed his eyes at her, and they moved past her, searching her room. "Yes, I am home. Are you alone?"

Just at that moment, the roof of the Jeep came into view as Sean coasted it out onto the road, and Sky felt the blood drain from her face. When she looked up at her father again, his skin had turned purple.

"LILY!" Gui had half turned toward his own room, showing a rather impressive vein throbbing in his temple. "Lily, *venez ici!*"

"Dad, please! Let me explain . . . but wait, why are you yelling for Mom? I thought she was with you at the police station all night?"

Gui stared at her in silence for a long moment, too angry for her words to make any immediate sense. Finally, he shook his head. "She left to come home and see that you were all right more than four hours ago. She is not here?"

Sky could only shake her head. Gui barreled downstairs to the telephone. "Lily, please call me at once. I'm worried that you aren't home yet, *mon coeur.*" Gui replaced the handset, standing over it in silence for a minute like he was willing it to ring. Then, to Sky's surprise, he picked it up again.

"Holly? It's Guillaume Rousseau. My wife left Oakridge Station more than four hours ago and hasn't been heard from since then. Are you able to contact your colleagues at the station . . . she was . . . yes, I'll be waiting for your telephone call."

He hung up the phone, but left his hand on it as though considering who he might call next.

"Dad, what's going on?"

"I made the mistake of thinking I could protect you both against a madman." Gui balled his free hand into a fist and punched a sizeable hole into the plaster near the front door. It was rare for him to lose his temper, and Sky had never seen his rage turn into violence, not once.

Gui turned, and his face instantly softened.

"I should have known he would come back. But I didn't mean to startle you, *coco.* I'm sorry." Still, deep lines marred his forehead, the furrows of old worries resurfacing.

Sky went over and hugged her father's arm. "Please, just tell me what's going on. Are you talking about Gage?"

The shock was evident in Gui's face.

"You know of him?"

The muscles in his arm flexed. "I found out last night that he was the one behind what happened to me on my birthday. He knew what I was, Dad. What I would become."

Sky felt the moment of understanding pass between her and her father—the man who had raised her throughout her entire life, and whom she would always consider her father.

"Your mother told you?"

Sky nodded. "I more or less figured it out after I met Severin." Her father opened his mouth. "Please, Dad, I don't want to go over the why and how right now. I just want to know where Mom is."

The phone rang, interrupting them. Gui snatched it up.

"Guillaume Rousseau."

Sky tried to listen to whatever the other person said, but it was too quiet for her to hear. His mouth had hardened into a tight line by the time he hung up.

"Dad? What is it?"

"Officer Vega said your mother was seen with a man wearing a long black coat and a bowler hat outside the police station."

"Gage? But Mom wouldn't have gone anywhere with him—"

"He would not have asked her, *coco*. Gage, he plays tricks with the mind, bends the will to his own wants—"

"Dad, I know. I saw him do it with the Swivellers, had them acting like wolves to chase me off the pier. I'm betting he also made Felix Swiveller drive over the Point."

Gui nodded. "It would seem so. Old Moley recognized him, but could not believe it was possibly him. We all thought Gage had disappeared forever after the fire sixteen years ago."

"How did Old Moley know him?" Gui gave her a faint smile. "Oh. He was in the circus, too, huh?" She couldn't imagine what the crusty old cur would look like in a leotard.

"I have not a clue where she could be, *coco*. Could you . . . does your gift work at all like your mother's? Could you find her, do you think, if you touched something of hers?" He grabbed one of Lily's scarves from the coat hook and held it out to Sky. She took it from him, even as she shook her head and her heart sank.

"If it does, I don't know how to do it."

But she did know how to *go* to her mother. Even as the thought occurred to her, light maps threaded through her brain and into a million, trillion pathways, weaving in and out of each other in every direction. Space, time—all intersected in a giant multidimensional spiderweb, with her mother pulsing blue as Sky sought her out.

"Skylar? What are you doing? Skylar, no!"

But Sky's father's voice was a distant rumble as she faded from the Blood House and reappeared a mile or so across town, in the ruined husk of the circus. The early morning breeze made Sky regret not getting dressed, and she hugged her bathrobe tightly around her. Her feet chilled instantly in the stiff grass growing through the ruins, but Sky picked her way through the debris toward the sound of her mother's voice.

Sky caught sight of her just as the oddity of what she was hearing sank in. Her mother wasn't talking to *someone*, she was talking to Sky.

". . . never wanted you to have that life, you see. I wanted *better* for you. So when I found out about you I had to get out, and I knew Severin would never leave Gage, couldn't leave the circus behind . . ."

Lily sat with her legs tucked under her, one hand plucking idly at the charred grass that had already left dark stains on her dress. Gage stood next to her, a terrifying figure in his long black coat and bowler hat. His hand rested on top of Lily's head, but his eyes bored into Sky as she stepped slowly into the tattered remains of the Big Top.

"And he wouldn't have let me leave, either, if he'd known about you. So Gui and I made a pact: we would run away together, leave our life with the circus behind once and for all, because he truly loved me, you see, not like Severin."

Sky had to swallow the rush of spit in her mouth as her stomach threatened to revolt. Seeing Lily's dazed expression, hearing the distant quality of her voice, Sky was in no doubt. Whatever tricks Gage was able to play with people's minds, he was doing it now to her mother.

Sky forced herself to take a step toward the unnatural tableau. "Mom?"

Lily's gaze never wavered. She continued talking softly, as though she were lulling herself to sleep.

". . . never stood a chance once Gage knew who they were. He took the skull, used it against your grandfather, made him do unspeakable things. Gui has always maintained he never started that fire, but I wouldn't have blamed him if he *had* done it, out of vengeance. Gage deserved to die. He stole so many children, so many."

"Mom, Gage isn't dead. He's standing right next to you."

The only response Sky received was a terrible smile from Gage. His teeth were yellowed, his mouth a cesspool that they had rotted in.

"I should never have run, never have gone with them, but Severin was so charming and I was just a girl, I didn't know any better."

"Mom, please snap out of it now. You're scaring me!"

"You couldn't *not* look at him. He was like a flame, he shone so brightly."

Sky took one more step toward them, but Gage stopped her with a shake of his head. Still, he said nothing.

"What are you doing to her, you freak?"

It was the worst insult Sky knew, but it only made his grin widen.

"Freak freak freak freak freak freak freak freak freak."

Sky stared at her mother. Lily's head tilted slightly so that she was staring right back at her daughter, her lip curled in an ugly snarl as she chanted the word over and over again. Then Lily smiled sweetly.

"All I want is one little thing, precious girl. Just a little thing, and then you and your mother can go back to playing house with the strongman. Wouldn't you like that, precious one?"

A chill ran up Sky's spine and she felt her lip tremble. The words had come from her mother's mouth, but that wasn't her voice. The patronizing look in her eyes wasn't Lily Rousseau. It was Gage.

"What do you want?"

"Ah, ah, ah!" Lily said the words in a mocking tone, but it was Gage who wagged his finger at her. "You should have taught her better manners, Lilith. I would never have allowed such insubordination."

Sky clenched her jaw, willing the creep to get to the point and ask for whatever it was he had turned her life upside down to get.

"I gave you time, precious girl. I could have brought about this marvelous awakening of your gift much sooner, left you bouncing between dimensions as a wailing toddler."

"*He's lying*," Jared said, suddenly standing next to her. Looking at Gage, Sky expected him to react somehow, to be startled, perhaps, but he gave no sign that he was even aware of Jared's presence.

"I'm only here inside your head, Sky." Jared moved as though he was about to hold her hand, but his fingers passed right through hers. *"Don't say anything, or he'll know what I'm doing."*

Sky darted a glance at Jared but said nothing, hoping he'd take that as a gesture of compliance.

"And now the pathways are yours to explore! How wondrous is that?"

Manic glee glinted in Lily's eyes, and Sky had to look away.

"He only waited until you were sixteen because Severin told him it was impossible for a child to become a Pathfinder," Jared said. *"That's the only reason he waited. He'll use you to get what he wants, and he'll never let you get away."*

The mime was playing games with her. Sky's temper flared. "Tell me what you want, Gage. Please, I'll do whatever you want me to do, just let my mom go!"

"I had hoped to keep this friendly, but you've inherited your mother's impatience. It's a very simple thing, really." Gage took his hand from Lily's shoulder, and her eyes cleared for a moment. As soon as they connected with Sky's, she screamed.

"Run, Sky! He'll use your power—"

But before she could finish, Gage's skeletal fingers flexed over her shoulder, and Lily's face became a blank. Then she looked at Sky with those not-Lily eyes and smiled.

"It is an amber ornament, a little bigger than my fist."

"You mean the skull?"

Sky almost bit through her own tongue. She had been so terrified that Gage wanted something to do with *her* anchor that she had blurted her question without thinking. Gage smiled.

"Yes, child. It belongs to me, and I want it back."

It doesn't belong to him, it's Severin's. Sky was wise enough not to say it aloud, but she still wondered, what was so important about the skull that Severin had been willing to die for it?

"What will you do with it?" she asked instead. A creeping dread seized Sky. Would he rebuild his circus with the Blackfin population? Would her parents become his puppets again, trapped in a traveling circus with all his other victims?

"Bring it to me," he said, using Lily's voice. "And your mother may still have some shred of her sanity when I release her."

Sky glanced at Jared, communicating with him silently.

"Tell Dad where my mom is."

❧ 29 ❧

THE PATHWAYS SPREAD outward in all directions, seeming endless at first, until Sky organized the strands and found the one she was looking for.

The last known whereabouts of the skull.

It had been at the circus, after little Jimmy had lost control of the wolves, and the Big Top erupted into chaos that even Gage could do nothing about. But then, he hadn't had the skull—Severin had taken it back.

So the skull really does amplify his ability to control people.

Even as the unsettling thought occurred to her, Sky grew lighter, and was pulled toward the last place she'd known the skull to be.

She expected to find herself among the throng of rioting Blackfinites who had been at the circus for what Sky guessed had been its final performance. Instead she materialized in one of the smaller tents.

Her heart lurched at seeing a blanched white face staring at her. But this face was not the gaunt specter of Gage, it was only a creepy clown face painted onto a wooden board. Other props were stacked all around her, creating deep shadows that looked ready to swallow Sky whole.

She took a few moments to study her surroundings, seeking out any other figures who might be hiding in the shadows. The circus bells were chiming discordantly, as though they knew the uproar going on at that moment inside the Big Top. Shouts and screams from the people jostling to get out of the tent reached Sky from a distance, and for a moment she wondered whether she was actually just hearing the echo of it through the pathways.

Severin appeared next to her, the tiny boy clutched to his chest, still unconscious. Severin himself was panting as though he had run to meet her. "Good, you found it all right, then."

Sky could tell Severin had no idea she had traveled back to her life in the present since their last encounter.

"What's happening in there?"

"The last I saw, Gage was having one heck of a time trying to fend off some of the locals. Seems that not having his favorite bauble has quite a debilitating effect on his mind-juju, if you know what I mean."

"What about my—what about Gui and Lily?"

In truth, Sky hadn't seen them on her last visit to the Big Top, but there had been such a crowd that she could easily have missed them. And despite knowing, logically, that her parents had escaped the fire that night, being back in this moment in the past made everything seem less certain. If Sky changed something now that led to them dying, she knew she could still return to her life in the present and find them there alive and well, but the possibility that she might create a timeline where her parents were no longer a part of the world—that would be something she couldn't live with.

"They're long gone by now, if that great oaf has a lick of sense."

Severin grinned at Sky, and she couldn't help but smile back at him. Even after all she had learned about him from her visits to the circus and her mother's memories, there was something about Severin that Sky couldn't help but take comfort in. Maybe it was their shared talent, or maybe it was the promise of the answers he held.

But that would be gone forever after this final visit to the past. Sky knew that the circus itself would be a burned shell after this night, and that Severin and little Jimmy would be gone along with it. But for now she had to ignore the heavy feeling in her chest, and the fact that she would never get the chance to know her biological father. That Jimmy wouldn't get the chance to grow up.

She needed to get the amber skull and get back to her present so she could save her mother. Her gaze zeroed in on the pocket of his coat, where the shape of the skull was noticeably absent.

Ah. So Severin didn't come directly here, either.

"Your amber skull, where is it?"

Severin's eyes lost their playful glint. "Now why would you be wanting that, *chère?*"

There was a noise like a gunshot, and both Sky and Severin moved to the flapping opening of the tent to see what had happened. Maybe fifty feet away from where they stood, the Big Top tilted briefly before settling back again. Flashing lights shone in and around the striped tarpaulin as people fought to get out, or simply fought each other in their panic. A high-pitched howl sounded, and Sky realized the wolves were still in there, somewhere.

No wonder they're panicking.

Of course, even their sharp teeth and claws were no match for a throng of rioting humans.

"Severin, I need you to trust me. I know it's like a family heirloom or something, and I wouldn't ask if it wasn't important. Please, give me the skull."

The boy stirred in Severin's arms, and he readjusted his hold on him.

"You wouldn't be returning it to Gage, would you?"

Some flash of acknowledgment must have shown on her face.

"Did he send you to wheedle out my secrets, then?" Severin laughed, but it wasn't the pleasant thrum of laughter she was used to hearing from him. "I shoulda known it was no coincidence that I'd suddenly find another of my kind."

"It's not like you think, Severin." He gave her an incredulous look. "Yes, Gage sent me to get the amber skull. But I'm only doing this to try to save my mom!"

Severin's mouth had been open, ready to argue with her. Now it snapped shut with a click of teeth before opening again. "Your mama? Another Pathfinder?"

"No, I told you neither of my parents are." Again, Severin appeared to be about to disagree with her. "I mean, the ones who raised me. I only found out yesterday that my dad's not my real dad."

Severin studied Sky for a moment, the distant sounds of the Big Top going into meltdown still escalating, but everything happening just a few yards from them felt a hundred years away.

"And your mother, is she a lady I might know?"

Sky nodded once. She could see the lines beginning to join together, the connections forming in Severin's mind.

"You aren't meant to be here, are you, *chère*?"

Sky shook her head. Words stuck in her throat; they would speed along this final encounter with the man who was just beginning to understand the connection between them.

"My present is sixteen years in your future. Give or take."

"Give or take." Severin smiled wryly. "And the man you've called your papa—that'd be Guillaume, am I right?"

"He's my dad, yeah." A moment, a look so searching Sky almost had to break away. "But so are you."

Severin's mouth set in a firm line, and he reached out a hand to brush her hair away from her eyes.

"I should have seen it," he said and shook himself, a smile creeping at the corners of his mouth. "It seems Miss Lily gave me a lagniappe, didn't she? But these wonderings are for another time. You need the skull, you said. I've hidden it—"

"Gampa!"

Little Jimmy, now very much awake, squirmed in Severin's arms, pointing with one pudgy finger to the field in front of them.

Gage moved through the darkness as though his feet barely connected with the ground, the brim of his bowler hat almost hiding the painted pallor of his face, but not his furious expression.

Severin swung the tent flap closed. "Run, *chère*. Out the back of this tent and around to where my trailer is—do you remember?—then you need to crawl under the end nearest the door. Reach up, and you'll find a small box. The skull is inside. Quickly!"

They both looked at the small boy, whose lower lip had started to tremble, and Sky reached for him. Severin shook his head.

"Leave Jimmy, he'll be fine. Gage might be twisted, but he'd never hurt his grandson. Go."

"But he—"

"Go!"

With one last look, Sky darted behind a stack of crates out under the tarpaulin of the tent. She looked around as she straightened, checking that Gage hadn't skirted around the back of the tent, but she could see the dark outline of him disappearing through the flap Severin had just closed. She was alone.

Sky ran, cold stinging her feet, keeping her eyes on the ground in front of her so she wouldn't miss her footing. She almost missed the darting figure heading the opposite way, hair trailing behind her. Hair so red that even the silvery moonlight couldn't diminish it.

Miss Schwarz!

Sky had no time to wonder if there was anything else she could have done or said to help the little boy. This night had already played out, the events creating their own pathway for Sky to navigate straight back to her present. That was where she could still make a difference, still save her mother.

Only a few more feet, and she was safely tucked into the shadows between the trailers where the performers stayed, and Severin's was within sight. She dropped to the grass at the end of his trailer and scooted underneath.

The great spoked wheels cast long fingers of shadow, pointing farther under the compartment where Severin had first told her that she was a Pathfinder.

Sky lay on her back and felt along the underside of the trailer. Cool metal and patches of rust stung her fingers, but there didn't seem to be any nook big enough to secrete the skull.

Just as doubt entered her mind, a flash of yellow light showed her where the box had been tucked just behind the fender. Everything was silent for a moment, and then terrified screams rang out over the unmistakable roar of fire.

Sky tugged the box free and crawled out from underneath the trailer.

Oh God . . .

The flash of light had come from the Big Top, but all around the central structure, smaller tents and kiosks were now burning with a fury, trails of smoke rising up into the night.

The tent where Sky had left Severin with Gage and little Jimmy was burning, too, and for a moment she was torn. This was the past, and she couldn't change the events of this timeline any more than she could change what had happened on the night of her birthday, but if she saved Severin now, she might create a new pathway where he survived the circus fire.

Cradling the small box with one arm, Sky sprinted back across the field to the tent, now hardly recognizable. The outer tarpaulin had all but disintegrated, and what remained was swaying dangerously in the wind, sending sparks out to fizzle against her bathrobe. Still, she stepped closer, shielding her eyes against the heat with her free hand.

"Skylar, get out of here!"

She could hardly see Severin for a moment, but caught sight of his upper body sticking out from beneath a burning crate. Her heart plummeted.

"Where's Jimmy?"

Severin coughed, choking on the smoke. "Gage got him out. But get you gone now, *chère*!"

Sky almost darted forward, but the whistling descent of one of the tent's support struts stopped her. A moment later, the blazing metal beam impaled the ground where she'd been standing.

"I can't leave you like this!"

He didn't answer for a long moment, and Sky started to panic that he'd lost consciousness.

"You're what's keeping me here, sweetness. You have my anchor!"

Sky could hardly hear his words over the roar of the blaze, but the moment she heard the word *anchor* she understood. By running back over to the burning tent carrying Severin's anchor, she had prevented him from escaping along one of the pathways, effectively trapping him inside.

"I'm leaving now!" she shouted, not sure whether he would hear her or if it even mattered.

Lightning threaded through her mind as the pathways opened up in a web around her and through her. And she saw her own anchor there, calling to her like a beacon.

Sky didn't even wait for the pathways to settle before she let her body become weightless, and she was traveling faster than light, faster than time.

❧ 30 ❧

SKY MATERIALIZED IN the seat next to Sean, and he screamed. He swerved before righting the Jeep and pulling over to the side of the road.

"Sky, where have you been? Is that soot?"

Sky, still catching her breath, looked down at her black-smeared and slightly sizzled bathrobe. "Uh . . ."

"And why can I smell cooked meat?"

"I'm afraid that is probably me."

Sky and Sean both whirled in their seats and found themselves face-to-face with a smirking—and slightly charred-looking—Severin.

"You *followed* me?"

Sky's eyes went wide. Severin was meant to have died in the fire, so he shouldn't have been able to travel to any point beyond that. His pathways should have ended, trapping him as surely as being near his anchor had kept him tied to that one spot in the burning tent.

Wait a minute.

Sky looked down at the box still clutched to her chest.

"I didn't have too many options, *chère*. You have my anchor right there." Severin nodded toward the box. Sky grinned, feeling a rush of unexpected joy at seeing him again.

"Uh, Sky? Who the hell is that?"

Severin crossed his arms and said, "Augustus William Severin the Third. And I'm her daddy, is who I am. Who in heck are you, son?"

"Severin, this is Sean. He's my, uh . . ."

"I'm her boyfriend."

Severin studied Sean for a long moment before turning back to Sky. "You could do better, *chère*. But in all seriousness, shouldn't we be saving your mama?"

When Sky looked at Sean, he was already restarting the engine, shaking his head slightly.

"Just tell me where to go."

✄✱✺✱✄

THE IRON GATES blocking the way into Blackfin Woods were no longer gates, per se, but more a mangled heap of metal flung to the side of the path.

"Looks like Jared found my dad," Sky said, and caught Sean frowning at her. "What's wrong? I mean, apart from the obvious."

"What exactly is Gage's agenda? I understand that his mind-control power is amplified by the amber skull, but so what? Why does he need it so badly?"

Sky had no answer. Severin, however, did.

"Gage is drawn to powerful objects, always has been. It's one of his talents, I suppose. But it's also necessary for him. Without other powerful people around him, he has nothing to manipulate, nothing to control. So he surrounds himself with gifted folks like us, keeping us on a leash while he keeps searching for more powerful objects to leech off of.

"He broke into my home in New Orleans the same weekend a traveling circus came to town. I don't know if he'd already gotten his hooks into the troupe, or if that happened later. But anyway, he demanded I give him the skull, in that special way that he has." Severin smiled thinly. "The skull had been passed down through generations of my family, and I wasn't about to just hand it over. It's a conduit for great power, stemming back to the very first Pathfinder.

"When the authorities tried to arrest Gage he used his power to manipulate the circus performers into helping him escape. And by helping him escape, I mean murdering a whole mess of folks. Since then, he's kept on using their gifts to line his pockets while protecting him at the same time."

"Is that why he started kidnapping kids, like my dad?"

Sky saw Severin nod in the reflection of the rearview mirror.

"Guillaume was eleven when Gage spotted him in Belle Dame du Pont—this lanky kid who was so clumsy he couldn't have hidden his strength even if he'd wanted to." Severin laughed. "He wasn't the first, but he was certainly Gage's favorite for a while. But Guillaume had too much spine for Gage's liking. He'd gotten dangerous, and by the time his folks showed up at the Big Top, I reckon Gage was really starting to worry."

"So Gage killed Dad's family to try and keep him in line?"

The shock on Severin's face was unmistakable.

"He did what?"

"He killed them. My mom showed me what happened—Gage went to the house and used his mind-trick thing to make my grandfather go postal. He killed his whole family."

All the color had drained from Severin's face.

"*Chère*, I had no idea . . . poor Guillaume. I didn't know Gage had gotten so twisted."

Sean kept his eyes on the path in front of them. "Because the kidnapping and mind control weren't enough?"

Severin laughed. "I've changed my mind, daughter. He'll do."

The Jeep trundled into the woods, following the narrow path which had once been a track leading to the church and the circus beyond.

"Oh my God, what is he doing?" Sky leaned forward in her seat, horrified and transfixed by the sight of her father, a dark silhouette among the ruins up ahead, brandishing what appeared to be a spear aimed at Gage's face.

Her mother sat with her back against a metal tent pole and her hands folded in her lap. Gage was either still controlling her, or whatever he had done had left Lily in some kind of trance.

Above the sound of the Jeep's engine, Sky heard her father shout something and saw him launch the metal post he had been holding toward Gage. Except it struck the ground nowhere near where Gage stood.

"Gage is skewing what Guillaume sees," Severin explained, leaning forward to watch. "He'd never have missed otherwise."

Sky remembered seeing the hulking figure of her father the first time she had traveled back to the circus. He had been throwing hatchets at a spinning target at the time.

"We should call Aunt Holly." Sean slid his cell phone from his coat pocket and handed it to Sky.

Seeing Severin's questioning look, Sky explained. "Sean's aunt is a police officer." The look changed to one of horror.

"Skylar, you do understand that if the police come and find your papa attempting to murder an old mute fellow in the woods, it's not likely to look good for Guillaume?"

"But Gage murdered his parents! And the Swivellers, too. And kidnapped all those people for his circus."

Severin looked at her levelly. "Prove it. As ringmaster, I was the one the police thought was behind it all. And Gage always made sure the circus moved on before the police could catch up with me."

Sky and Sean exchanged a look before he took back his cell and slid it into his pocket.

"So what do we do when we reach them?" They would reach the clearing in a matter of seconds. "If Gage can mess with our minds, how can we get him to let your mom go?"

"He said he'd let her go once I hand over the skull," Sky said quietly, but she knew Gage would have no reason to keep his word once he had it. He could simply brainwash them *all* if he wanted to.

"It will mean I'm tied to him again."

Sky's heart sank. Of course Severin would be chained to Gage if she gave up Severin's anchor. He'd spent years under the mime's thrall, and now he was about to be put in exactly the same position— only now he was sixteen years in the future.

Could Sky really exchange Severin for her mother? Even if she barely knew the man, she couldn't deny the connection she felt to him.

The Jeep skidded to a halt just short of the first twisted tent pole. Gui had wrenched another pole from the ground, and swung it like a bat to try to hit Gage instead of throwing it at him.

"He still can't see where Gage is," Severin whispered next to her. Sean stood at her side and chewed his lip.

"One of us needs to distract Gage so the others can get Mom out of there."

"I'll do it," Sean offered. Severin rolled his eyes.

"No, it's better if I do it. I'm valuable to Gage, so he's less likely to do something . . . unpleasant. If this doesn't go well, give him the skull. I'll think of some way to get it back later."

Shaking his head like he couldn't quite believe what he was doing, Severin crept around to the far side of the ruined tent before entering the rough circle of the remaining tent poles.

Moving as stealthily as they could, Sky and Sean made their way to Lily. Sky heard her mother humming softly to herself.

"Hold up there, would you, Gui? I'd rather not have you hit a home run with my head."

Severin strode into the center of the circle, his arms held wide—the consummate showman. But Gui had already spun to see who had spoken, and with his momentum the metal pole came swinging around.

"Dad! No!"

All three stopped and turned to look at Sky as she ran toward them. Gage's face twisted into an ugly grin.

Gage held out his hands to her, one beckoning her forward, the other waiting for the skull. The trees at the edge of her vision seemed to lean in, and the world became distorted. The next moment, she was standing in front of Gage, placing the box in his outstretched hand.

His smile was triumphant.

Sky tried to move, to turn to look at her father and Severin behind her, but it was as though the command didn't reach her limbs. All she could see was what was right in front of her: Gage's vile grin, his deft fingers sliding open the top of the box, the crooked pole where her mother had been sitting moments earlier.

Lily was gone.

Thank God, Sean got her away!

Gage held the amber skull in his hand, its grin mirroring his own. If Sky had been in control of her body, she felt certain it would have been convulsing under the weight of Gage's power.

"Grandpa." Sky couldn't turn to see who had just run into the clearing, but she recognized Jared's voice, even out of breath. "Stop what you're doing!"

Something hit Sky from behind, and it took her a moment to realize it hadn't been anything touching her physically. Some force was pushing back against the hold Gage had over her, until she was able to stumble back, away from him. She rushed to her father, who was still frozen with the metal pole inches from Severin's face. She twisted the pole out of his grip and it thudded to the ground.

Gage looked furious when Sky turned back to see what was happening. He gripped the skull with white knuckles as he faced his grandson, but Jared stood his ground.

Despite the dyed hair, Sky could see it now—Jared's eyes were the exact same shade of gray as little Jimmy's had been. He was taller than the old man, his shoulders hunched with whatever he was doing to counteract Gage's power. But he was shaking with the effort, and Sky saw that he wouldn't be able to keep it up much longer. She needed to free Gui and Severin from Gage's thrall and get them out before Jared lost the battle.

"Get the skull!"

Jared's voice screamed inside Sky's head, and she ran at Gage. He was so fixated on his grandson that he only saw her at the last moment, and the world spun as he tried to disorient her. But Sky was already on top of him.

A woman screamed, but Sky couldn't see who. It hadn't sounded like her mother.

Flailing almost blindly, one of Gage's gnarled hands wrapped around her throat before her hand connected with the cold amber. It thudded to the ground somewhere nearby.

A ten-ton weight pinned her to the ground, pushing her down until she could neither move nor breathe. Crushing, suffocating, breaking.

SEAN'S ARMS HELD her, not crushing like the ugly weight of a moment ago. Glancing around, Sky thought nothing had changed in the clearing while she'd been dazed. But then she saw it had been long enough for Gage to pick up the skull and knock Jared out with it. An ugly gash showed the spot where the skull had connected with Jared's, and his eyelids didn't even flutter as Gage leaned over him.

Gage looked up at the woman's scream, and Miss Schwarz glared down at him from the roof of Sean's car with her hands tensed like claws.

"I knew you'd come back! As soon as she reappeared and I saw she'd become like *him*"—she pinned Severin with her eyes—"I knew you'd want to use her to get to your precious amber skull. You're *still* so hungry for power, still obsessed with that damn circus! *After everything you did to me, to my Jimmy!*"

"Who's that?"

Sky jumped as Jared's astral form appeared next to her just outside the ring of tent poles. A glimpse inside the ruined structure showed his body still lying unconscious next to Gage, whose eyes were fixed on Miss Schwarz.

"Uh . . . I think that's your mother."

"Sky, who are you talking to?" Sean peered at the spot where Sky was looking at a very wide-eyed Jared, but he of course saw nothing.

"Jared. I'll explain later."

"You let Jimmy die!" Miss Schwarz raised her hands and a great plume of fire rose from the ground in front of her. It curled and twisted in the air, forming a giant ball of flames.

The orange glow made Gage look even more demented. He held the skull in front of him, but Miss Schwarz swept her hand toward him, sending a tendril of fire streaking across the space between them. It wrapped around his arm like a lasso, and the skull rolled free into the grass.

From where she stood, Sky saw Severin's eyes follow it, though neither he nor Gui could move to pick it up yet. Except that Gui *was* moving.

"You started the fire, Jani. All that followed was your doing."

Sky's heart raced at hearing her father's voice. It sickened Sky to hear it being used by someone so twisted.

"You took him from me!" Miss Schwarz shrieked, and the fire wrapped tighter, higher up the mime's arm. Gage's face twisted in pain.

Sky looked up and found Jared staring at Severin.

"How the hell is *he* here? I thought he'd died in the fire," Jared said.

"Severin's my father. I sort of accidentally brought him with me from the past."

Jared's astral form disappeared from where he had been hovering next to her, and a second later Sky saw him roll over and groan in the clearing, back in his own body again.

"It was you, Jani. You killed him."

The look on Gui's face as he taunted Miss Schwarz would have broken her heart had she not known Gage was behind it.

Seeing his chance, Gage lifted Jared by the collar of his jacket with his free hand, and held him up like a shield. Jared blinked dazedly as the fireball surged in front of him.

"Miss Schwarz, stop! You'll kill Jared!"

Miss Schwarz paused at hearing the terror in Sky's voice, but not for long. "What do I care, Skylar? I tried to warn you."

So that explains the note. "But he's your son! Jared *is* Jimmy!"

As one, every person in the ring who could move turned to look at Sky as she stepped forward.

"My boy died in the fire! He was too little to control it, and I was too late!"

The woman's face crumpled with grief as she sank to her knees on the roof of the Jeep. Still the fireball moved toward Jared and the man cowering behind him.

Sky understood now. "He didn't. Gage made you believe you'd seen him die so he could keep him from you."

Miss Schwarz's cry was deafening as the truth hit her. The fireball swelled as her rage fueled it.

"Miss Schwarz, don't! You'll kill them both!"

Jared was conscious enough now that he struggled against Gage's hold, trying to get out of range of the fireball that pulsed hotter, stronger, as Miss Schwarz lost her grip on it. She screamed and the flames surged forward.

No!

Sky's voice was lost to the lightning wrapping around her. The pathways pulsed brightly, and she seized the strand she wanted and dematerialized.

She was weightless for the briefest instant until she emerged, close enough to Jared to yank him away from Gage's grip. Sky felt the burn of the fire above where they lay in the grass, engulfing Gage in a roar of fury, grief, and loss. That was the only sound as it swallowed the man who could utter no cries of his own.

Miss Schwarz slipped from the roof of the car and wept, crawling toward where Jared lay staring at the man who raised him burning in the ruins.

Sky was lifted into Gui's arms, her father's mumbles in French making no sense to her.

"What about Mom?" Sky asked.

Sean answered next to her. "She's awake, but doesn't seem to know where she is. We should probably get her to the hospital. Jared and Miss Schwarz, too."

Sky felt Gui nod against her hair. "You are a good boy, Sean Vega. As reckless as my daughter, but just as brave, too."

Gui set Sky on her feet again, and she swept one final look around the clearing as Gui held open the car door for her.

"Wait, where's Gage's body? And where did Severin go?"

Though the flames lingered on the ground, there was no sign of the man they had seen burning moments earlier. An ugly, impossible thought occurred to Sky.

"Oh God, did he just make us hallucinate that? Did we just see what Gage wanted us to see?"

The sound of another car engine firing in the distance seemed to confirm it.

But where did Severin go?

Sky slid into the passenger seat next to Sean, Gui taking the backseat with Sky's mom in his lap, and Jared and his mother squeezed in next to them. Jared and Miss Schwarz held on to each other in silence, both looking like they were suffering from shock.

"If Severin has the amber skull, *coco*, that's who Gage will go after."

Sky knew her father meant to reassure her, but the thought of Severin being hunted by the demented mime gnawed at her. She watched in silence as Blackfin Woods fell away behind them, then Blackfin itself was hidden behind the towering peaks of the Lychgate Mountains.

❧ EPILOGUE ❧

SILAS SPUN ON his axis, the unoiled metal screeching in a most obnoxious fashion. A shift in the air had drawn the weathervane's gaze, dragging him away from some very deep thoughts on the unnatural properties of Saran Wrap. When he stopped spinning, the dark line of the pier was in front of him.

Not this again. He sighed.

There were no bells this time. The girl materialized three feet from that other Pathfinder—Severin, if Silas remembered correctly—and leaned against the same guardrail that had splintered under her hands almost six months earlier. She steadied herself, as though still unused to her parlor tricks.

The smoke from Severin's cheroot wafted up toward Silas, who rather hoped the man would choke on the vile thing. As it was, he didn't, so Silas was forced to eavesdrop on their conversation instead.

"I was just standing here wondering when you'd figure out how to find me."

The girl sat on the boardwalk so that her legs dangled over the edge. After a moment, Severin sat next to her. Side by side, it was easy to see the two were related in some way, even if Silas had not just seen them both emerge from some secret pocket of the universe.

The two were so magnetic—doubly so when they were both in the same spot—that he had little choice *but* to watch them.

"Your message was kind of hard to ignore when it appeared in the woodgrain of every door in the house!"

The man graced the girl with an enigmatic smile. "Your home was most obliging. But you still had to decipher the map to find me here." The smile faltered. "Tell me, how is your mama?"

"She has good days and bad days," the girl said. What Silas realized, even if the girl didn't, was that her mother was now much closer to his side of the veil than theirs. "Are you going to kill him, if you find him?" There was a long stretch of silence where Severin did no more than suck on his cheroot and stare out over the ocean. "I heard you threatening to kill him the first time I traveled to the circus, you know. Who were you talking to?"

"I have threatened to kill Gage many, many times, *chère*, but I was probably talking to Madame Curio when you overheard me. But to answer your question, yes, I plan to kill him. Gage will never let us be while he lives. It is so tiresome having to constantly watch one's derriere when we should be out unraveling the mysteries of the universe."

The girl shook her head. "Not me. Now that Gage is off searching for you, there's really no reason for me to use the pathways anymore."

"Are you telling me that despite being able to navigate the cosmic pathways, which are barred from every other human being, you can't think of a single reason why you might want to utilize this gift? Ah, but I suppose you have glee club and cheerleading and such to be getting on with, *chère*."

She kicked the leg dangling next to hers.

"I get your point, old man, but it's weird. And scary."

Severin laughed his musical laugh. "*Life* is weird and scary, *chère*. And yes, so is pathfinding. But both are gifts to be explored, and we each have our safety net." He gestured to the gothic-looking walking cane leaning against the guardrail, on top of which gleamed some kind of amber ornament. A skull, possibly, though Silas found the idea rather distasteful.

"And what if we lose our anchors? Didn't you say we'd be left drifting through the pathways, not able to find our way back to our real lives again?"

"Ah, but there's a way to make sure that never happens, little daughter."

"What's that?"

Severin rose from the boardwalk, twirling the cane in his hand. "Why, you carry your anchor with you, of course. Took me a while to figure it out, but it's possible, *chère*. Pretty much anything's possible, if you want it enough."

Silas would have frowned down at them both if he'd had the brows for it. *She almost unraveled the whole town,* he thought. Such secrets weren't to be trifled with, especially not by some slip of a girl.

"You never did tell me why the skull was so important to you. I mean, before Gage took it from you."

Severin held the leering thing up in front of them. "Now that is quite the story, chère, and one I always used to love hearing from my own papa. You see, the first Pathfinder lived over a thousand years ago, and he was not the smartest shrimp in the bayou. A so-called friend made him a wager that he couldn't use his gift to steal the beating heart from the Tree of Life. . . ."

The weathervane resumed his spinning, caring little for the absence of a breeze or the two figures blinking out of existence on the pier beneath him a short while later.

Silas had bigger things to think about.

MY THANKS

Because they were the first *Blackfin Sky* readers, I thank them first: Jani Grey and Erin Fletcher, who ask all the right questions.

The writing friends who have made me a better writer (and my journey far more fun): Bridget Shepherd, Cait Greer, Misty Provencher, Summer Heacock, and Ian Hiatt.

Those who suffered through my early writing attempts, and urged me to keep going: my sister, Alex; my mother, Julie; my best sounding board and aunt, Gabrielle. Also my dad and stepdad, who have encouraged and supported my every writerly adventure.

Molly Ker Hawn, my brilliant agent, who believes in my writing and makes others believe in it, and who helped me shape *Blackfin Sky* into something weird enough to be wonderful.

Penny Thomas and Janet Thomas at Firefly Press and Lisa Cheng at Running Press Teens, who held my words up to the light and polished each one to a gleam.

And thank you, always, to Ian. I wasn't a writer when he married me, and he came along for the ride anyway.